DANGEROUS CURVES

What Reviewers Say About Larkin Rose's Work

Kiss the Rain

"In this story Larkin Rose has created two awesome leading women who in their own way tower over everyone. I was truly dazed at the beginning and continued to be astounded throughout the novel. ...I can, without a doubt, recommend this book for the extraordinary strength and stunning depth that each noteworthy woman presented to me over and over again. Transcendent! [The conclusion] sent me soaring and believing in miracles. This book is like ambrosia and a nearly perfect kiss among Eve, Jodi, and the rain. Incredibly satisfying!"
—*Rainbow Book Reviews*

"Even if you're not a fan of erotica, Larkin Rose is an expert at knowing how to keep you turning the pages. *Kiss the Rain* is the story of what happens when Jodi and Eve meet during London's Fashion Week. It also tells how lives can change in seven days. The sex is extremely hot, and the tension is high. This is an enjoyable read which is perfect for a beautiful spring day."—*Just About Write*

I Dare You

"Rose's well-crafted debut novel is erotica with benefits—plausible plotting, a fast pace, and well-defined secondary characters, including an engaging gay drag queen whose sturdy shoulder is always there when Kelsey needs grounded queer advice."—*Q Syndicate*

No Leavin' Love

"This story feels like an allegory and from that viewpoint it soars, dips, spins wildly around its central theme, and certainly touched my own heart's periodic desire and longing to go home. These are two powerfully impressive women, who pretty much met their match between them. I certainly recommend you stay the course, enjoy the wedding, and then discover when or how the loose ends get resolved. Marvelously pleasurable!"—*Rainbow Book Reviews*

Visions

"Past intertwines with present in Rose's (*Kiss the Rain*) charming new erotic romance. Fortunately, the seduction unfolds with enough spice and sweetness to keep readers satisfied."—*Publishers Weekly*

"I howled, applauded, panted, and dabbed away the tears from pure pleasure while reading this book. This is a wonderful multi-layered love story, peppered with nearly devastating confusion, and practically undermined by misunderstood class collision. I think it would be divine to see this as a play or movie, but the remarkably pure sexual heat would definitely limit the distribution venue. What a shame. At least there is the written word and that has masterfully unraveled the intimacy and details allowing me to savor the humor, the women, and the monumental obstacles seeking to crumble the wishes and desires for the star-crossed characters. I unquestionably recommend this!"—*Rainbow Book Reviews*

Vapor

"This story possibly takes the ultimate award in having two people completely misconstrue each other. Plus, they never talk about it. Of course, with the super sizzling action between the sheets, on the staircase, in the washroom, who really has time to discuss anything? Brilliant, engaging, funny, tearful, and loaded with love, I was beguiled from the very beginning. Hats off to Larkin Rose, another Bold Strokes Books author, for masterminding this marvelous book."—*Rainbow Book Reviews*

Visit us at www.boldstrokesbooks.com

By the Author

I Dare You

No Leavin' Love

The Pleasure Planner

Vapor

Kiss the Rain

Breaking the Rules

Dangerous Curves

DANGEROUS CURVES

by

Larkin Rose

2019

ISBN 13: 978-1-63555-353-6

This Trade Paperback Original Is Published By
Bold Strokes Books, Inc.
P.O. Box 249
Valley Falls, NY 12185

First Edition: April 2019

CREDITS
Editor: Cindy Cresap
Production Design: Susan Ramundo
Cover Design By Jeanine Henning

Dedication

To the readers. Every word on every page
is for your enjoyment. I hope the "behind closed doors"
scenes put a smile on your face. Or better yet,
on someone else's. You're welcome!

And to Rose. Always.

CHAPTER ONE

L acy McGowen backed up to the headboard and tightened her grip around the black iron bars. She licked her lips in eager anticipation while her date, a groomswoman from the wedding hours earlier, her name long forgotten, if she ever knew it at all, kicked off her shoes and eased onto the foot of the bed.

She'd found the woman standing alone at the cash bar toward the end of the reception, mixed drink in her grasp, holding Lacy in her gaze as she walked through the crowd to capture those forever moments in her lens. Locked in that gaze was exactly where Lacy had desperately needed to be. She'd been dealing with an hysterical bride most of the day, making it almost impossible to take the pictures required for such a lavish wedding.

This meaningless, never going to see you again sex, was the only bonus in her otherwise headache inducing and sanity testing job of being a wedding photographer. She hated it. Hated bridezillas and their redundant demands. Hated the orderly fashion and statuette poses.

But it was the lesser of two evils. The greater evil being her passion, a passion she couldn't think about without memories rising to snag her breath. Without leaving her nauseated and trapped in her own fear. Those testy brides and squealing bridesmaids were far from the roar of a race car engine, from the stench of racing fuel, and the adrenaline of capturing the win in her lens, but it was where she now felt safe. The only place she felt safe. Those impossible to deal with people were her hiding place.

Her date crept closer. As if those sexy dark eyes hadn't been luring enough, the accent that poured out over the woman's invitation to join her for a drink absolutely sealed the deal. It had been so enticing, so soothing while they made small talk, while Lacy finally felt some relief from a long day of dealing with the unruly bride who whined her way to the altar. From her last-minute change of hairstyle, to her pouting over adding two pounds to her already ridiculous one hundred and nine pounds, which sent the mother and bridesmaids into coddle mode, cooing what a beautiful bride she was, to stop calling herself fat.

Lacy had silently agonized her way through it all, envisioning stomping her own feet like an unwound mother in the middle of a meltdown. But her hands were tied if she wanted to keep her job, the company she'd started after she left NASCAR, if she wanted to stay in Los Angeles instead of going back home to that Podunk town of West Virginia where she was born, where her parents still called home when they weren't road-tripping across the map in their RV, where she would likely land a job wrestling toddlers into group settings and making silly cross-eyed faces at unrelenting infants.

Her date climbed higher, her eyes serious and focused. Yes, she had told Lacy her name. Rachel? Monica? She'd also shared where she'd been born. Australia? New Zealand? If only Lacy could remember. Not that it truly mattered. Not that it ever did.

The woman slithered forward, and strands of short brown hair fell around her forehead.

"Stop," Lacy commanded.

The woman gave her a smile and inched her hand up the comforter to prove she would only half listen to Lacy's orders, that she was a bad girl and would reverse the roles if push came to shove.

Lacy's insides tightened with the knowledge. She liked the bad girls. Wanted the bad girls. They played by their own rules. They were usually incredible in bed. Sex. It was just sex. Simple sex.

"Take off my boots." Lacy stretched one leg toward her. "And tell me your name. Again."

The woman's gaze moved up her leg, between her thighs, across her breasts, before landing squarely on Lacy's face. "The part of your body I need to taste doesn't require the absence of your boots. My name is Zoe. Again."

Okay, so Zoe and New Zealand sounded kind of similar. At least she was close.

Zoe moved closer.

Lacy pressed the toe of her boot into her chest. "Easy, tiger."

"Is that a request? To be easy?" Zoe pushed Lacy's leg out of the way and crawled higher. "If I remember correctly from our little conversation, you don't expect things to be easy."

Ahh. So Zoe had been paying attention during their three-shot meet and greet when Lacy had actually complained about her hectic job. Damn. She'd done that. Complained. She hated that. That she'd whined or bitched or loosened her tongue. It was such a buzzkill being on the receiving end of such boring nonsense. Nothing was a bigger turnoff than listening to someone bitching while trying to muster up a nightly fuck.

She made a mental note to apologize very soon. With her tongue.

Despite the fact that she'd allowed liquid courage to almost change the outcome of her night, Zoe was here now, obviously undeterred, and ready to please.

Zoe grabbed Lacy's hips and jerked her down the bed. "What would you like me to do to you?" She placed her hands on either side of Lacy's head and lowered her mouth to Lacy's lips. "Your wish is my command."

Lacy expelled a sexual sigh as she settled beneath the tight body.

"Make me come." That was her only wish. To just be taken away for a few minutes of blissful spasms.

A sexy grin swept across Zoe's lips. She balanced herself on one hand while she moved the other between Lacy's legs. She palmed her crotch and squeezed.

Lacy moaned.

"Making you come would be a simple task." She squeezed once again and then bucked against her own hand. "Simple isn't the core of such an exquisite being, is it, Lacy?"

The way the accent lured her, Lacy was tempted to say no, that there was nothing simple about her, nor did she want there to be. Right now, she just wanted to agree with everything Zoe was saying.

Fact was, she'd love to endure the simple things in life. As hard as it was to admit, she'd even take a little simple with her sex. Normally, sex was fast, hot, and a slingshot to the point. It had to be. She had little time for games or the normal get to know you routine. Order a drink, capture the willing gaze of a handsome butch, followed shortly with a "Your place or mine?" That was her normal.

But every once in a while, long lasting sex wouldn't be so bad. It'd be welcomed, in fact. What was it like to wake up beside someone? What was it like to roll over and look into someone's eyes who actually loved her? What was morning sex like? Sleepy good mornings and roaming lips, while the sun kissed the world awake. That's what she wanted. Deep down, it's all she'd ever wanted.

Zoe snagged open Lacy's jeans and tugged them down her thighs. She locked the denim around her boots and looked up with a satisfied expression. A brief smile crossed her lips before she ducked under the tunnel of denim, lifted Lacy's legs around her neck, and fastened her mouth around her clit.

Lacy instinctively bucked against her face with the suction. She fisted one hand in the comforter. The other in Zoe's hair.

Zoe licked and sucked, lapping, mumbling, teasing, until Lacy arched off the bed and came in a blind fury of wet sex.

She pumped against Zoe and hissed out her release until her body went still.

Zoe eased out from between her legs. "Told you those boots wouldn't be in my way. But they might be now." She pulled off one boot, then the other, and finally tugged Lacy's jeans off her body.

Lacy wanted to resist. Normally, that orgasm would have sealed the end of their night together. But the expression on Zoe's face promised so much more. What could a few more minutes hurt?

Lacy was game for an encore. She deserved it. Wanted it.

Zoe hovered above her. She was truly a sexy creature. Not to mention that accent more than likely turned smart women stupid. She was a great catch. A great catch to someone looking to snag someone.

Lacy wasn't that person. She was only looking to snag the next gig. The next photo shoot. The next bridezilla. And then what? Continue running from those images. That's what.

How much longer was she going to run from her demon? That ugly, vivid demon.

The question dredged a memory free, and Lacy focused hard on Zoe, willing the images to leave her in peace tonight.

"On your knees, *tiger*," Zoe said, ripping Lacy out of those dreadful thoughts. "But first, let's uncover the rest of this perfection."

Lacy sat up and allowed Zoe to remove her shirt then her bra.

Zoe's gaze dripped over her hardened nipples, down the flat of her stomach, then snapped back to her face. "Such a shame."

Before she could question Zoe's statement, she rolled Lacy onto her knees. She folded Lacy's hands around the iron bars and kissed the nape of her neck. "Hold on tight, my lovely." She trailed a finger down Lacy's spine, over the cheek of her ass, into her wet folds, teasing, circling. "Enjoy the ride."

She kicked Lacy's legs farther apart and teased her opening again.

"Do it," Lacy mumbled, past the need for more relief.

She didn't have all night. In fact, Zoe should already be headed toward the door, if not beyond it. Lacy's greed, that accent, those promise-filled eyes, were the only reasons Zoe was still here now. It was time for their night to come to a halt.

She didn't do sleepovers. Didn't wake up spooned with a lover.

Relationships were outside her realm of specialties.

Lenses, zooms, backdrops, and those damn impatient brides. Those were her perfection. Actually, now those were her perfections. But not then. Not years ago. But now, unfortunately, it was.

There it was again. Creeping back in. The memories. Those awful images.

"Now!" Lacy demanded, desperate to chase the snapshots back into hiding.

Zoe teased her clit, and Lacy arched back with a moan, pleading with her posture. Begging for satisfaction with the sound alone.

"My my," Zoe said and then pushed inside.

Lacy hissed and drove backward, fucking herself over those pleasing fingers.

Zoe drove deeper, faster, pushing Lacy toward that magical place where she could be controlled, where she let her guard down and gave herself entirely. Where chaos didn't exist. Where demanding clients couldn't reach. Where scenes of death were forbidden.

She heard the distinct sound of a zipper growling right before Zoe pulled one of her hands from the bar. She pushed it between her legs. "Help me. You are torture."

Lacy slipped her fingers through slick folds, stalled long enough to tease her pebbled clit, and then pushed inside her.

Zoe's hips hitched forward, and she drove her fingers deeper.

From somewhere in the room, a cell phone chirped and then rang out the personalized tone, "*Billy the Badass Anderson calling. Billy the Badass Anderson calling.*"

Lacy ignored the sound and drove faster over those fingers, pushing inside Zoe at the same time.

"Is that Billy Anderson? The race car driver, Billy Anderson?" Zoe asked.

"Don't stop!" Lacy growled, drawn into the sexy sound of her accent, mentally cursing Billy for screwing with her sex time, hating that the whole damn world knew her best friend was a real badass.

She loved Billy, God knew, but his timing still sucked after all these years. From his hardcore fights with his dad about his need for speed on the back roads in high school, to his heartbreaks with his girlfriends in college, that man was still calling her at all hours of the night to be his shoulder to cry on, his venting post.

Now he was a married man, dad to the most precious little girl alive, racing career under his belt, and yet her phone was still the one he dialed at least once a day.

Of course, she knew why he was calling tonight. He was anal about keeping Lacy on track, wanted to make sure she'd packed her bags, that she would make it to the airport on time for her month-long vacation with him and his adorable family, like she did every year during NASCAR down time. He knew her so well. God love him.

No matter the reason he dialed her number, no matter the why, she was always there for him. She'd loved him from the second he had copped a feel with her in their graphic arts class, in the dark room when he thought he was safe, and got his nuts kneed up into his throat. He was the spoiled high school quarterback who did nothing more than bat those baby blues for a passing grade while she struggled through every project, getting pathetic scores because she rode the wild side when the instructions clearly stated that mild was the intention.

Screw mild. She didn't want mild. She wanted naked flesh and bad girls. She wanted racy wardrobes and parted lips. She wanted action. Which is exactly why she couldn't score a passing grade to save her life. No matter her plea, no matter her argument, her teacher waved her away with a demand to fix it every single time.

And here she was, running from herself, locked in the only career that could keep her close to her passion for photography and far, far away from the action, the death—his death—that made her run far, far away to begin with.

Somehow she'd managed to escape the class with a credit on her high school transcript, but it'd been by the hair of her chinny chin chin. And her relationship with Billy had begun the second he hit the floor bellowing in pain. All these years later, he was still the love of her life.

The phone went silent while Lacy's orgasm curled tight.

As if summoned, Zoe reached between her legs and flicked her clit.

"Yes." Lacy drove inside Zoe, feeling her slick walls tighten around her fingers, and then her orgasm jerked her into spasms.

Lacy cried out while Zoe's hips jerked. With a hiss, she fell across Lacy's back. They ground against each other for several minutes until they both slid down to the mattress.

"Wow," Zoe whispered into the back of Lacy's head.

The phone rang out again, and Lacy growled out her aggravation. "Seriously? Someone better be bleeding or in a coma."

She crawled across the bed and dug through the pile of clothing until she found her jeans. With a huff, she jerked the phone from the pocket and connected the call.

"Is my princess Gabby in a hospital?" she barked.

There was silence for a split second before Billy answered. "Nope."

"Is that beautiful wife of yours bleeding?" she asked, notching her irritation, even though Billy would only mock her aggravation.

She loved that about him. How he never took her shit. How he could solve her problems from thousands of miles away with his voice alone. How he always let her be herself even if he didn't agree with a damn thing she was saying. Especially when he didn't understand a single thing she was bitching about.

He was such a jock. He understood football. He got the logistics of baseball. He lived race cars. But when it came to women and love and all the drama in between, his brain went void. She loved that even more about him.

"No," Billy said.

"Well, it's obvious you aren't dead. That means you have absolutely no reason to interrupt my…" Lacy rolled onto her back and eyed Zoe. Zoe quirked an invitational brow at her. "Extracurricular activities."

"You couldn't keep it in your panties long enough to pack your luggage, could you?" Billy joked.

"I don't wear panties."

Zoe leaned over and placed a kiss against her ankle. "I can attest to that." Her gaze cut up to Lacy, and she placed another kiss higher.

"I'm hanging up, Billy." Lacy licked her lips while another kiss moved higher.

"No, you won't. You're my biggest fan," Billy said.

True. She was. He was the love of her life. The thought of ever living without him in her world made her ill. Made her mentally buckle. Which is why she couldn't watch him race. Why she couldn't read the tabloids. Why she couldn't even watch the news. Okay, so she occasionally snuck in some tidbits, but watching a race was completely out of the question.

Worse, her best friend was one of the biggest names in NASCAR. His life was on the ledge every time his engine roared to life. Through every blistering curve, his life balanced. Every wreck, every blown motor, every blown tire, his life was at risk. The lousiest part, it was Lacy who finally gave him the strength to stand up to his father, to demand that he allow Billy to go after his own dream. It was like she pushed him into that reckless career. If anything ever happened, she knew she would never forgive herself. Ever.

"You're about to get a whole month of me in less than twenty-four hours. What is so pressing that it couldn't wait?" Lacy slid her leg wider while Zoe climbed higher.

His silence snagged her attention away from Zoe's pleasing lips. He never missed a chance to bust her balls unless he was in his feelings.

"Tick tock," Lacy said, watching Zoe's fingers slide up her legs.

"I need a huge, gigantic favor from you," Billy finally blurted out.

"Huge *and* gigantic?" Lacy squirmed while Zoe pressed a kiss inside her knee. "Gabby would hurt your feelings right now for using two words that have the same definition."

Billy chuckled. "That she would."

"So what huge and gigantic favor do you need from me? While on vacation, don't forget." Lacy widened her legs as Zoe's kissing climbed higher.

"A racer needs a little, um, revamping? I'm using Darlene's word."

Lacy arched a brow at his words. Billy never asked her for favors that included anything to do with racing. He knew better. And if his wife said it was revamping, that only meant that whoever it was was a total loser and needed a complete overhaul. "A racer?"

"Yeah. No one you would know." He paused, which was a red flag. He always paused when he was dodging the truth. "Fresh photos. Maybe a new wardrobe. Plug a few things into social media for publicity. That sort of thing," he added quickly.

"Uh-huh." Zoe's kisses were inches from Lacy's crotch, and her insides clenched. "It's Sebastian, isn't it?" Lacy's head swam with the thought.

Sebastian Andre was the biggest egotistical jerk-off Formula One had ever known. He'd advanced into the NASCAR world only two years ago. She'd had the misfortune of meeting the bastard while vacationing with Billy. His forward advances had been blatant and gross and not in the least bit arousing, if a man could arouse her, that is. Any woman who found his despicable flirting flattering, was either desperate or an idiot. Or both. A horny high schooler had more respect than he did.

Worse, her subtle refusal had only stirred his need to score. Was it every man's dying wish to turn a lesbian straight? For sure it was Sebastian's.

"Sebastian? Of course not. But would he be the worst client you could think of?" Billy asked, a hint of excitement in his question.

"I'm not responding to that. As big of a prick as he is, there could be worse." She could think of a few others, but then she would have to admit that she had indeed picked up a few tabloids—or more—while at a doctor's appointment, and read the highlights of the newest rookies. One being a woman, which should be exciting for NASCAR and women all around the world, except she had already stirred enough drama to get suspended before her first race. For sure she wouldn't be back, which was great because Billy was gullible enough, and loveable enough, to take her under his wings and begin mechanically attempting to fix whatever mental issues she had. He was just special like that, thinking he could fix everything and everyone. That he could fix the world.

And then there was the British man, also second year in NASCAR, who had already caused a wreck due to irresponsible driving, and promised the new season would start with a bang. Zoe nipped the inside of her thigh, her hot breath feathering against Lacy's crotch.

"I would never ask you to—"

"I know," Lacy said, terrified he would say too much. The memories were already nudging. "I love you."

Zoe pushed Lacy's legs apart and slowly teased her clit with the tip of her tongue.

"I love you, too, hotrod."

"See you at the airport. Gotta go!" Lacy tossed the phone on the bed, wove her fingers into Zoe's unkempt hair, and held on.

CHAPTER TWO

Kip Sellars, known to most as Sellars, to the rest, Asshole, downshifted and turned into the on-ramp. The convertible top was open, filling the car with cool night air. For now, the space beside her was empty. She hoped to fill that vacant passenger seat at the next nightclub. The bar she'd just left offered slim pickings for what she was looking for tonight. An easy lay. Yet not too easy. She didn't want a drunk falling into everyone's lap. Nor did she want the one girl the entire bar had already fucked. Something in between. A girl that would give her a little eye teasing while she kept her distance. While she waited for Sellars to take the first step. To take the lead. But at two in the morning, that would be hard to find. Hours of party life would ensure most of the ladies were already too drunk or had already been taken. Hopefully, the next club would provide what she so desperately wanted tonight.

The roads were practically empty. Peaceful. Where she could be one with herself. Alone with her thoughts. With her demons. Just the way she liked it.

She pushed the pedal, and the '69 Yenko Camaro obeyed with grace by smoothly surging forward. The motor purred in acceptance as she merged onto the highway.

The speedometer slipped past seventy, seventy-five, eighty. Without encouragement, the images of her past flooded her mind. The speed of the back road race of her past, the adrenaline for the finish line, and Sarah's laughter as she stood in the opening of the sunroof, her arms outstretched to the night sky, head thrown back, begging Sellars to go faster, faster, faster. She was the most beautiful creature Sellars had ever known. Magnificent to the core. Daring, yet simple. Sharp-tongued, but sweet like the sound of waterfalls. She was everything. She had been Sellars's everything.

Sellars pushed the pedal harder as the harsh images stabbed at her mind. Eighty-five, ninety. The guy she'd been racing, Mark Hammonds, was two car lengths behind her. Where most people normally landed when she raced them. She was good. Speed didn't bother her. It enveloped her. She'd been born to be behind the wheel of a race car. Behind the speed of mustangs. There was no adrenaline rush higher than when the world was a blur around her.

The memories pulled her deeper. To Sarah's shocked scream. And then to the deer darting into view.

Her heart had skipped as she instinctively slammed the brake and jerked the steering wheel hard to the right, away from the large beast. The sound of tires squealing bounced and echoed against the pine trees lining the road. Both cars skidded into a spin. Round and round, the world had spun around her. And then the incredible sound of crunching metal as the car slammed to a stop.

When she awoke, screams filled her mind. Far away. So far away. A male. Bellowing. Not Sarah. Sellars had opened her eyes to a film of red. Warm liquid poured from her scalp and down her cheeks. Pain wrenched her chest as she attempted to look around.

Realization slowly crept in as Mark's voice grew louder, clearer, panicked.

Pinned against the steering wheel, Sellars focused on the passenger seat. A single shoe lay against the fabric. Sarah's black pump.

Sellars's heart jammed as she attempted to shove against the steering wheel. Pain wrenched down her back. "Sarah!"

"Don't move, Sellars!" Mark yelled from beside the car.

Sellars struggled to look around at him. His T-shirt was blotched in blood, and a crimson line ran from a gash across his forehead.

"And for God's sake, don't look." He choked out a sob as his gaze swung toward the front of the car for a brief second.

His soft-spoken words were nothing more than an invitation. She craned her head against the shrilling pain in her head and ribs to look out the shattered windshield.

Across the hood, lay Sarah. Her beautiful tanned legs reached back to Sellars. A single black pump rested against the crumpled hood. A lone headlight gave enough light to the scenery. The front of the car was embedded in a tree. And so was Sarah.

Sellars growled with the memory of her own screams, of the pain those screams evoked, and jammed the pedal to the floor.

Eighty-five, ninety, ninety-five. She entered the Fort Pitt Tunnel of Pittsburgh on a blur. The engine's whine echoed against the curved concrete walls as she reached one hundred miles an hour. The speed, the wind, the sound and feel of the power beneath her, always pushed her deeper into her memories. Closer to Sarah. She clung to the pain of that night. She deserved it.

She'd killed Sarah. She'd killed the love of her life. All for the sake of a cheap thrill. All for the sake of Sarah's laughter. To give Sarah what she wanted. She wanted the speed as much as Sellars had. What she wouldn't give to have her back. To hear that sweet voice once again. To curl up in her arms beneath that old oak tree on old man Harris's farm overlooking the pond. They used to skinny-dip there. They made love there. So many times. There they'd made plans for their future. Sellars would do as her father expected. She would go to that nose-to-the-sky college and study medicine. Sarah would follow. She could be a waitress, maybe a bartender. She didn't care what she had to do as long as she could be with Sellars. Sarah hated school. Despised books and exams and people. She hated people the most. But God, how she loved Sellars.

And in between all the studying and tests and cramming information into her brain, the weekends could be spent on the racetrack, doing what she knew Sellars loved the most.

"Give your parents what they want because they love you in their own controlling way. Be happy you have someone who cares about your future. But love yourself just as much. When school is over, you can go after that racing career."

It was touching how she thought the world worked like that. How she truly believed that Sellars could do both. That she thought school would be over in a flash, degree in hand, and that she could walk away and step right into a racing career. If only the world were that simple.

Fact was, Sarah had no one but the grandmother who took her in when no one else wanted her. She wasn't forced to go to school. She wasn't forced to abide by curfews. She had no clue that in twelve years, possibly longer, her window into the racing world would be gone. Not to mention, with all of her time being spent with her nose in a book, there would be little to no time left to race, even if only for fun. Especially for only fun.

"And you'll climb higher. To NASCAR. And you'll be a doctor and a badass race car driver. We'll have the perfect life. And I'll be waiting for you right there, where the flags drop, every, single, time. Because I'm yours until I take my last breath, Miss Sellars."

Sellars burst through the opening in the tunnel to the breathtaking view of Pittsburgh across the Monongahela River. The images of that ugly night faded as she took in the beauty of the night lights. The pain eased with the silhouette of the high-rises. She backed off the pedal, coasted across the bridge, then took in several calming breaths.

Desperately, she needed that nightclub. That woman. That fuck. A woman who would make her forget her ugly past, if only for a little while. Even though it was hypocritical. She liked being close to those thoughts. Close to the memories of Sarah. The good ones. The tranquil memories of better days. Of the only good days she had.

She knew that wasn't true. She'd had great days. The day she walked away from college and confirmed she was the true black sheep of the family, knowing her father would never speak to her again. The day she packed her duffel bags and left the dorm without saying good-bye, Pittsburgh bound, on the heels of Mark, who was the only person who could understand her disturbed behavior because he'd witnessed her turmoil in all its ugly glory. The day she signed up for racing school. All the days of winning races. The first day she raced for Formula One. And the day she was accepted into NASCAR, and then arrested four days later, and then suspended before she could ever put her feet on the asphalt.

Yes. Suspended. For street racing. And if she didn't keep her nose out of trouble during the down time, she might never set foot inside another race car.

She cared about that. Her career. Having it stripped away by some suit and tie who didn't know a damn thing about her, pissed her off.

If only she could care what others thought of her. She couldn't think less of herself after what she'd done to Sarah, so their opinion mattered very little to her. They hated her rough style of racing. They hated her aggressive behavior on the track. Their hatred made her more reckless. As long as they hated her, they would leave her be. And that, they did.

Of course, their desire to stay away from her had more to do with her reputation off the track. She was a bad girl. Cared about very little. Thought of no one but herself. And wasn't a stranger to handcuffs.

Jailed for drunk and disorderly conduct several times, street racing, obviously. It didn't help that she'd been caught in the alley beside a club with her hand up a woman's skirt. Turned out to be a racer's wife. A NASCAR racer, of all things. How was she supposed to know who the woman was? How was it her fault he wasn't living up to his expectations in the bedroom? He should have thanked her instead of promising war. Sellars wasn't the only person his unhappy and unfulfilled wife had been screwing. She surely wouldn't be the last.

But now she was on the shit list. Despite the fact that her grandfather was one of the biggest sponsors in NASCAR. Her biggest sponsor. Only one of three decals left decorating her car.

She should have known no one would take her serious. Should have known they would never believe that she'd gotten herself to where she was, without him.

She'd given up her family to wear that helmet. She'd raced her way into Formula One. All by herself. She'd even stayed when she never really felt like herself, or even comfortable. She had a mission, and a goal, and her uneasiness paled in comparison to reaching that checkered flag.

And then one day she was invited to a NASCAR party on the Bristol track in Tennessee where the guys would take their wives or girlfriends for a light spin around the track for brownie points. For scoring rights.

The sound of those engines was like music. The scream of the tires almost magical. And when one of the racers tossed her a helmet and encouraged her to take a turn, she fell in love.

From the second she felt the vibrations of the car hum through her body, she knew NASCAR was where she wanted to go from there. Where she wanted to call home. Where she wanted to take the next step, despite the pitfalls that move would bring.

So she went out for a qualifier and was accepted.

Well, that was until they suspended her. They knew she was a bad girl before they offered her a spot on a team. What had they expected?

Now the choice was, shape up or move along. She couldn't blame them even though she didn't know what her personal business had to do with her racing record. So what if she lived on the edge? So what if she wanted to take a married woman to bed? So what if she wanted to drink herself into the corner of a back alley? What did that have to do with the checkered flag? What did that have to do with winning?

According to them, the suits, her behavior meant everything. She was a role model, under a new organization. She had to abide by the rules.

Screw that! She didn't want people to look up to her. She didn't want children to dream of being just like her one day. She just wanted to race. Wanted the speed. To forget. Or not to. She wasn't sure anymore.

Other than her few sponsors, her grandfather being the main one, Sellars didn't care about anyone. Especially herself. Until she met Billy Anderson at her first NASCAR fundraising event, where she would meet the other racers, where Brett had promised she hadn't seen the last of him, that when she least expected danger, the danger would be over.

Yeah. As if his punk ass worried her.

That event was one of the few she was allowed to attend, and Billy was the only person to even shake her hand.

He didn't look at her with disgust. Didn't stare or gossip like a child. He'd walked right up to her, hand out, and told her she was going places, that it might take her a while according to the route she was taking to get there, but she would get there nonetheless.

She'd been so shocked by his words of encouragement, having never heard them from another living soul except Sarah. Her parents had assumed she would follow their medical path. The path she'd started and just couldn't finish. It was expected, actually. Her brother and sister had followed that engraved route, so why wouldn't Sellars? They had never told Sellars they were proud of her for going after her own dreams, for winning races, for doing a good job. Why would they? Her dream was against the Sellars family itinerary.

Billy's clap on the back had brought tears to her heart. Had made her feel like a child needing that kiss on a boo-boo.

They became fast friends, and she adored his family. His wife, Darlene, was a sweetheart. She especially adored their only child, Gabby. She was the most outspoken child Sellars had ever known. Not that she'd known too many. She normally didn't take too well to kids. She couldn't get down on their level enough to enjoy them.

For weeks, Billy had been giving her racing tips in between raving about his best friend, Lacy. The way he talked about her, the woman walked on water. She was a photographer in Los Angeles, specializing in weddings. Sellars had been shocked to learn that she was the photographer who had captured Doug Nealey's death. A fact she was sworn to keep to herself. Billy claimed the subject was off limits, and Sellars vowed to keep that promise now that he'd offered Lacy's services to Sellars. It would be Sellars's comeback, he said. A new image, he declared. If anyone could do it, it was Lacy.

He practically insisted, leaving Sellars feeling like she didn't have a choice, that she might honestly hurt his feelings if she didn't accept the offer. When she brought up the idea to her grandfather, he'd clapped, said Lacy had been a top-notch photographer and he was willing to pay top price to ensure she would take the job of keeping Sellars on the right track until the end of her suspension.

As much as she wanted to refuse, as much as she wanted to just sit back in her naughty corner and wait for NASCAR to lift her restrictions, she was more scared of losing her dream. She'd clawed her way here. She deserved to be here. She'd be damned if she let anyone stand in the way, even if that person was herself.

Sellars eased to a stop at a red light and shifted the gear into neutral. Baby, the name she'd given her beloved Camaro, vibrated in protest. She wanted the speed as much as Sellars wanted to give it to her. She was covered in a sleek magenta, trimmed in chrome, and she loved her master. The faster Sellars pushed her, the more she begged for more.

Sarah had pleaded for the same thing. The speed.

"Faster, baby! Put this bitch in the wind!" she would scream from high above the sunroof, her favorite spot with every back road race.

She'd been so wild. Sellars missed her so much. Eleven years and counting, and there wasn't a day that went by she didn't think of her, yearn for her, or hear those cries of release in her mind.

An engine revved beside her, and Sellars looked to her left to find two guys staring back at her. The driver revved again in invitation.

"Ahh. Now we're talking." Sellars gave them an approving nod, pushed in the clutch, and shifted the stick into first.

Her heart quickened as she padded the pedal. Baby roared and vibrated, eager for the juice.

The hand on the crosswalk blinked six...five...four... three...

Sellars tightened her grip on the steering wheel. Her insides tightened as well, reminding her she needed to finish this kid off and get to that club. She needed to fuck so bad it was painful.

Two...one.

Sellars punched the pedal and popped the clutch out. Tires screamed as they both surged off their mark with the green light. She floored the pedal, and Baby obliged. Three seconds, Baby swallowed thirty miles an hour. Sellars quickly shifted into second to keep up with her thirsty need. Forty, fifty. Her insides clenched as she pulled away from her competitor. What a dumbass. Her well-tuned engine could wipe the ass of almost any contender. She shifted into third. Fifty, sixty. Adrenaline rushed down her limbs as she shifted into fourth. Seventy, eighty. Damn, she needed skin against her. She needed to drive into someone. Needed to come over their fingers. The need was too strong. This win even stronger.

Ninety. His headlights were in her rearview mirror, and she smiled. It was a view she was very accustomed to. The view of winning.

Blue lights slashed through the night sky from a parking lot twenty feet ahead of her. A cop.

"Dammit!" Sellars pulled her foot off the pedal.

Great. Another night in the slammer listening to drunks talk about their experiences with aliens from outer space or how their homes had been bugged by the government or that the world was really flat.

She passed the cruiser about the same time her competitor slowly passed her. Asshole.

Sellars didn't bother with a blinker as she pulled into the first empty parking lot she came to. The only thing she could hope for now was that a pretty lipstick lesbian would approach the car. One that would ask for her license and registration with pouty lips and flirty eyes. It had happened. Several times.

With a deep breath, she stopped the car and cut the engine then waited for what seemed like eternity for the officer to open the door.

He emerged from the car, all six foot three of him.

Yep, she was going straight to jail.

Forty-five minutes later, mug shot complete, Sellars scanned the room for a place to sit. It was the wee hours of a Saturday morning. Of course the place was packed with the weekend party animals who couldn't control their fun-filled actions. Like she couldn't, even without the alcohol.

She had four chairs to choose from. One beside a woman with her hair twisted into dreadlocks talking loudly to herself. Another vacant chair beside a woman with deep pockmarks and pimples all over her face. She repeatedly picked at them. Third choice was beside a tiny man with his head down. Sellars knew how he felt. If only she could hang her head and make the world go away. Last choice was a girl who couldn't be over the age of twenty-five, who was watching Sellars curiously.

Hmm. She was quickly reminded that she never got to that fuck.

However, picking up a lay in a club versus one in jail was quite a different story.

Then again, she was in the same place. Locked the hell up.

Against her own desires, Sellars chose the chair by the man. At least he would be quiet and keep to himself.

Now what? No way she was going to leave on her own recognizance. She'd already used that get out of jail free card. A few times. There were only two people in her life she could call. Her grandfather, who she wouldn't call if her dying breath depended on it. And Billy. It was comforting to know Billy would be there. Without a word, he would help. It was nice to know, right or wrong, he would come to her aid.

She didn't deserve for anyone to help her. Maybe one day they'd lock her up and throw away the key for good. Then she could live out her days in a cell with three square meals a day to wallow in her own self-pity.

Three hours and a shift change later, Sellars had settled into her chair with eyes closed and head propped in her hand when someone cleared their throat above her. She opened her eyes to find a pretty officer standing beside her. Who could forget Tanya with her dragon tattoo and nipple rings? She was damn slick at cuffing. And fucking.

"You just can't get enough of this place, can you?" Tanya teased her with a wink. "I was excited to see your name on the list when I came in for shift change."

Sellars shrugged. "What can I say? I don't know how to behave."

Tanya fingered the top of her cuffs tucked in her belt. "Well, someone should do something about that."

Yes. Someone should.

"So, have you had your phone call?" Tanya asked.

"No."

"The judge will be here in an hour." She pointed toward the end of the counter. "Go ahead and make your call."

"Thanks." Sellars stood, thrilled that Tanya let her gaze trip down her body. Too bad there wouldn't be time to take her up on the unspoken promise.

But right now, her career was hanging in the balance. A career she loved despite the ways she was demolishing it.

She'd been warned about her behavior. She'd been suspended to confirm they meant what they said.

Would this push her sponsor over the edge? Her grandfather. Would he finally pull her funding? Was she pushing him to do exactly that?

Had she screwed up? Again? This time for good?

Tanya led her to the phone, and with another wink, she went to look after another jailbird.

Sellars dialed the number before she could change her mind. She was embarrassed to have to call Billy. He'd been so helpful. So caring.

It was also comforting to know he'd come. She couldn't say the same thing about anyone else in her life.

"Hello?"

"Billy, I, um, need a favor."

"Sure. Name it."

She hated to say the next words. "Bail me out?"

There was a long pause. She could well imagine his disappointment. She deserved nothing less. He was trying to help her. Giving her the most honest advice. Treating her like she was a team member instead of a nobody. Hell, her own team was treating her like she was an enemy. Yet, she deserved that, too.

"I'm at the airport waiting for Lacy, remember? But I'll come straight there as soon as she lands."

"Thanks, Billy. I owe you one."

"A big one."

Sellars hung up the phone and made her way back to her chair. Great. Now she'd meet Billy's famous best friend right out of the slammer. What a way to make a first impression.

Her thoughts went to Sarah. Her wild child. Her sidekick. Her everything.

Gone.

Sellars was her killer.

She wasn't deserving of any kindness. Not from her parents. Not from her family. Not even from Billy.

Movement caught her attention. She looked over to see Tanya watching her.

Like she needed the demons to leave her in peace, she needed that fuck.

"Officer, I'm feeling a little queasy." Sellars groaned.

A quirk lifted the corner of Tanya's lip. "There won't be any puking on my tile today. On your feet, inmate."

Sellars resisted jumping up and speed-walking to the bathroom. Instead, she slowly stood and gripped her stomach.

"Let's go. Down the hall and to the right," Tanya said. "Larry, got a sick one. I'll be right back."

A middle-aged man with a beer gut and bald head barely lifted his gaze from the computer screen as they moved past his station.

Sellars obediently allowed Tanya to guide her into the bathroom. The door had barely shut before Tanya pressed into her. She hungrily kissed her. Tongue delving.

She suddenly withdrew and stared up at Sellars. "How would you like me, my sexy captive?"

Sellars managed a smile before she leaned her weight against the back of the door. "On your knees, Officer."

CHAPTER THREE

Lacy rushed for the escalator with her carry-on bag, anxious to get her arms around Billy. She missed him like crazy and hated that their visits were only once a year now that she was consumed by that thing called earning bill money. She needed more of him. More of Darlene, the sweetheart who had captured his heart, and definitely more of Gabby, Lacy's mini twin. More of this black-and-gold-breathing city.

Her work, his career, kept them both moving at fast clips in their lives. It sucked. And as if he couldn't give her enough by being the bestest friend a girl could ever have, he added Gabby to the list. She was eight, going on twenty-eight, and a tiny version of Lacy. All sass and class with a sarcastic wit that could cut a grown man down to size, and she happened to hold Lacy's heart in the palm of her hand.

She missed them all so badly it made her ache sometimes. Maybe it was time to do something about that.

Billy was standing at the base of the escalator, and Lacy's heart lurched. God, she loved that man.

That make you warm and fuzzy radiant smile lit up his face, narrowing his bright blue eyes into slivers of tropical ocean water. Overwhelmed by the need to get her arms around his neck, Lacy charged down the moving stairs. She reached the bottom, dropped her bag, and jumped into his arms, legs instantly locking around his waist. She dampened his cheeks and neck and forehead with heavy kisses.

"Goddamn, I missed you!"

"I missed you too, hotrod." He squeezed in return.

Minutes passed while people gave them loving smiles. They got that all the time. People mistaking them for a couple. Those expressions never bothered her. Nor did she ever set anyone straight. She didn't care what they thought. Fact was, she and Billy were perfect just the way they were, no matter how the outside world perceived them. People would never understand their deep connection. Hell, Lacy didn't understand the deep-seated love half the time herself.

How could a high school jock, who made a huge mistake of grabbing her ass during class, with his buddies egging him on, become her reason to breathe? It was unfathomable. Lacy hated guys. Hated them more in school. Most were jerks, and the ones who weren't were gay. Yet here they were, unbreakable, all these years later. He was far from a jerk. Far from gay. And loved Lacy as much as she loved him. It was incredible, and it was a part of her life she couldn't and wouldn't give up for all the riches in the world.

Billy set her on her feet and grabbed the duffel from the floor. He led the way toward the luggage conveyor. "Gabby has already called three times with the traffic report."

"Ahh, my princess. Always looking out for our well-being."

"I told her it was five in the morning, that there wasn't much traffic, and that she should stop worrying and go back to bed."

Lacy turned a scornful eye on him. "How bad did she hurt your feelings?"

"A little. A lot. She reminded me that she was eight years, ten months, and seven days old and if I would stop treating her like a toddler who couldn't tell time she could have already finished her update on the traffic. And then she told me to turn down that disgusting country music so I could pay attention."

Lacy laughed. "She's going to be the first woman president. Bet your sweet ass."

Billy groaned.

Ten minutes later, they were in the car and headed toward the freeway. Lacy took in the scenery. She loved Pittsburgh. Nowhere ever felt like home the way this beautiful city did. She loved the hype of football fever. The tranquil alone time at the Point. She especially loved the nightlife. A single girl could find all her heart desired in this Steel City. There was never a dull moment. Never a dull evening unless you chose it. She could see herself living here permanently. Again. Wanted that. A lot. Hanging out with Gabby every day would be so good for her soul.

Instead, she was still living in a place she couldn't stand, doing a job she hated, and she didn't know why. Billy had all but begged her to come live with them while she found work, maybe even start her own photography business that didn't include weddings.

"You could go back to doing those naughty shoots you used to love so much in school." He would always remind her. "You were good at it."

Those naughty shoots he referred to were the ones that almost changed her mind about staying in college. Her secret fetish of capturing raunchy, yet tasteful, images of naked women, revealing their true colors. There was nothing more breathtaking than seizing someone's personality. She could do that. She could create that moment, work it into a photo shoot, and freeze that image, that expression, that deep center, forever. And she had. A lot. Right before she fucked them. Sometimes again, right after, when she could capture that raw, you've been fucked expression.

Except the jobs had led her to the actresses and actors, the rich, the famous, all through word of mouth. It seemed she had simply traded demanding riches for hysterical bridezillas in the end. Those that were headed to fame could be worse than a frazzled bride at times. Dealing with them made her never want money.

Or if she was going to have it, she wanted to be just like Billy. Other than living in a gated community in a fairly large house, you'd never know the man had a fat bank account. He still drove an old pickup truck and loved the flea markets where the best bargains could always be found. And he was generous with his fame. He helped people. Gave money to charities, as well as his time. He was a damn good guy who felt blessed to have the life he did. Just another reason why she was so in love with him.

"We have a pit stop to make," Billy said.

"Hope it's quick. I just got a text from my precious angel asking if you were doing the allowed five miles over the speed limit instead of the illegal ten you normally do." Lacy giggled.

"I do not." He glanced down at the speedometer and then let off the pedal when Gabby's statement proved correct.

"I won't rat you out."

He gave her a brief glance with his lip curled. "Yes, you will."

She smiled. "Of course I will. That's my girl."

He smirked and settled into his five miles over the limit.

Several minutes later, he pulled off the exit ramp down into the heart of Pittsburgh. This never got old. The lights. The high-rises. The feeling of home.

"I know, before you say it, you love this damn place."

"I do." She pressed her face against the window to look up at the buildings. There was no other place like it.

Billy finally pulled into a parking lot, and Lacy looked out to see police cars.

"Why are we at the detention center?"

"Be right back." Billy quickly hopped out of the car without answering.

Lacy got out, leaned against the car, and lit a cigarette. A habit she'd picked up a few years out of college, after a grueling afternoon with a film director and part of his crew for a photo shoot. Or rather, those so-called people who were headed for fame. She couldn't even remember the name of the movie they had been shooting. They'd been the most unprofessional bunch of dimwits she'd ever encountered. Whining, bitching amongst each other about who should be toward the front, who should wear what outfit. It had been the most exhausting five hours of her life, and on one of their mini tantrum breaks, she'd found the quietest female of the bunch alone in the parking lot with a plume of smoke above her head.

"Those are bad for you," Lacy said, irritated but thankful to have a few minutes' peace away from those irritating voices.

The woman flipped open the pack and shoved it toward Lacy. "When I smoke one of these, those assholes live another hour."

Lacy took in her serious expression, then plucked one from the pack.

She'd been smoking ever since. Fact was, cigarettes gave her a natural calm. It was like having a Zen moment. Several lives had been saved with the flick of her Bic.

The doors to the jail opened, and Billy walked out followed by a very fit woman wearing stonewashed jeans and black blazer over a pale gray T-shirt. Her brown hair was a sexy mess. She looked like someone who had just crawled out of bed instead of released from a jail cell. Her hands were shoved in her front pockets and her head was down like the whole world was bearing down on her. Given that she was leaving a jailhouse, maybe that was true.

They approached the car, and the woman looked up.

Crisp green eyes met Lacy's. Wow. Kip Sellars in the flesh. She was more gorgeous, far more handsome, in person. The tabloid shots of her mischief gave no justice to the square jawline and stern posture. She was hot as sin. And knew it.

She was recently suspended from NASCAR before her very first race as the newest rookie. Or so the article in the magazine had said. She was reckless, hated by every other racer on the track, and appeared to not care about her behavior or the people around her who took offense at the bad girl. Had it not been for her nasty attitude, or sleeping with a married woman, Lacy would actually respect her desire to play by her own rules.

Hell, hadn't Lacy snubbed her nose at those who didn't like her style of photography many years ago? It wasn't in her nature to check other people's choices. Live and let live was her motto. But when it came to disrespecting the hand that fed you, she drew the line. That was exactly what this woman was doing. Biting the sponsors' hands. The few sponsors she had left on her side, if Lacy recalled the article correctly, were the only ones who saw potential left in her.

And that potential was incredible. She had a smooth grace on the track. A grace that made people notice her. A grace that had the rest of the pack at attention. They feared her. As well they should. If she could have gotten her shit together, she could have been one of the greats. Of course, she wouldn't share that knowledge with Billy, who believed that she stayed far, far away from the racing grapevine.

Sellars settled her sights on the beautiful Lacy. Billy's best friend. The one he couldn't stop rambling about. The very woman he had talked about like she was some kind of Egyptian goddess. Not far from the truth now that she was staring down over her. She'd never seen anything more divine, especially the intrigue floating in Lacy's brown eyes. Billy never mentioned how delicious she was. Wearing nothing more than a pair of skinny jeans, chocolate ankle boots, and a beige satin shirt hanging delicately off one shoulder. No bra. Her nipples strained against the fabric. Sellars mentally hummed with the thought of their hardness against her tongue.

She wanted to taste her. Dammit. She wanted it more than anything right this second.

How in the world was Darlene okay with her husband having such a luscious piece of ass for a best friend? It intrigued her. Fascinated her, in fact. In her world, women and men weren't best friends. They were either fuck buddies or constantly caught up in the jealousy of their spouses. There wasn't a middle ground. But in their case, they'd found it. Owned it. Cherished it.

Better question was, how would Billy feel about Sellars adding his best friend as a notch on her bedpost? God knew, she would. Soon. Very, very soon.

Lacy shifted to ease the sting of need between her thighs. Sellars was practically eating her alive in that carnal stare, deliberately inspecting her body.

She spoke just to break the gathering of wet heat climbing between them. "Ahh. Kip Sellars. I see the rumors are true. You truly do possess a fetish for orange jumpsuits."

Images of sexy poses flashed through Lacy's mind. A throwback black and white striped jumpsuit with the top half cradled around Sellars's hips, her wrists cuffed and crossed, hands covering naked breasts, with a fuck you growl on her lips. Another with her sprawled across the hood of a police cruiser, an eat my dust snarl dominating her expression, and her middle finger to the world.

Wasn't that basically what she was doing every time she got thrown in the slammer? Wasn't that the personality captured in every tabloid headline?

Oh, what she could do with that delicious piece of butch ass.

Billy cleared his throat. "Sellars, this is Lacy."

Sellars gave a curt nod, and Lacy felt a twinge of wet need stir between her thighs again.

"Lacy, meet Sellars. Your new client."

Lacy coughed with the sudden exhale of smoke and swung her gaze on Billy. "Over my dead body. You have lost your fucking mind!"

Sellars looked shocked as she glanced toward Billy. "You didn't tell her? That's sick, dude."

"Dude? You still say dude?" Lacy interrupted that comical stare. "That explains a few things."

"What explanations would those be?" Sellars crossed her arms.

Lacy looked over Sellars's shoulder to see Billy's pleading eyes. Damn him. "Nothing."

"Oh no. Don't back down now, cute thing. I'd love to hear the speculation about my life from a woman who tucked her tail between her legs and ran until the ocean on the opposite side of the map stopped her, who doesn't know a damn thing about me except the crap you read in those lying tabloids."

Billy grumbled in the background, and Lacy reminded herself to deal with his confession later.

She stepped forward, stirred by the mention of her past, or the reason why she'd ran.

"Ah hell," Billy mumbled.

"The whole fucking world knows all about you, Kip Sellars. You display your true colors so vibrantly, after all. You're a drunk, a womanizer, home wrecker, lawbreaker, albeit one of the best drivers I've ever set eyes on, with some sick, twisted need to sabotage your own career." She stepped closer, damned if she would back down or break down from those anger-filled eyes. "I couldn't give a shit what you do with your life or your desire to fuck it up. I don't give a rat's ass what politician's wife you fuck or what public place you choose to fuck her. I couldn't care less about your liquid poison habit or your illegal need for speed. What I do care about is Billy, his accomplishments, his reputation, and hanging out with the likes of you, having to come rushing to save your pathetic ass from a jailhouse, is sure to tarnish his pure image. That, oh twisted one, I won't tolerate. And I sure won't contribute to the delinquency of stupid by wasting my precious time on a hopeless case. Find someone else to polish your egotistical image because whatever you're paying won't ever be enough to work with a train wreck like you."

Lacy stood her ground while Sellars stared hard at her.

Billy had already hung his head.

"No amount of money?"

"Not even a million bucks."

A smile finally twitched on Sellars lips. "That's cool. It's your loss. But you're wrong about one thing, sexy."

"Just one?"

"She was a race car driver's wife. I detest politics."

"Fuck you."

Sellars took a casual step back, her smile half-cocked and sexy. "Wow. Billy was right about you."

Lacy lifted her chin. "Oh yeah? How so?"

That smile deepened. A single dimple cut into her right cheek as she leaned forward. "I call shotgun."

"I'm driving!" Billy blurted.

Lacy was left with her crotch a wet mess while they piled into the car.

What had just happened? Had she made it clear that she would have no part of this revamping bullshit? No amount of photo shoots or wardrobe changes could fix that woman.

She had said no, right?

Out loud?

CHAPTER FOUR

Lacy squealed from the back seat as soon as she spotted Gabby perched on the front porch in her Betty Boop bathrobe Lacy had shipped to her for her last birthday. The very one her daddy said was too teenagery for her. The exact reason Lacy bought it as well as the pajamas and slippers that matched.

She was a living doll with her hair up in a messy bun, her mama's striking dark eyes full of happiness, and her daddy's bright smile plastered on her face.

Her heart skipped as Billy finally came to a stop short of the garage. "Get out. I know you're dying," Billy said.

Lacy threw open the door at the same time Gabby bolted off the porch.

"Aunt Lacy!" Gabby ran across the plush green yard and jumped into Lacy's arms.

"My smartass angel bear!" Lacy feathered her face with kisses. "I have missed the living shit out of you!"

"See, Daddy. I told you it would take her less than five minutes to start adding to my college fund," Gabby said over Lacy's shoulder.

Lacy put her down and held her at arm's length, taking in the maturity already transforming her little girl features. From her long dark lashes to her flawless skin, she was beautiful. "Did you make him shake on that bet? And how much did you wager?"

Gabby gave her a big grin, and Lacy could almost see the incredible woman she would become one day. If only Lacy could protect her from every heartbreak she would endure until one person was strong enough, kind enough, and open enough, to endure the whirlwind she would likely be. "There are three things a lady should always keep to herself. Her love life, which I'm not allowed to have until I'm thirty-five because my daddy lives in the dinosaur age. Her income. Which means I can't reveal my profit."

Lacy kissed her cheek hard. "And the third?"

"Her next move. Never reveal your next move."

"That's my baby girl." Lacy pulled Gabby into the crook of her arm and turned to find Billy and Sellars on the sidewalk watching them, her luggage dangling from their grasp, a look of longing in Sellars's eyes. Her insides tightened at the blatant stare. "First female president standing right here. Better grab your autographs now, losers and gentlemen. They'll be worth a mint years from now."

Gabby scoffed and bumped Lacy with her hip. "Don't be ugly. Sellars is cool."

"Sorry, kiddo." She let her gaze slip down Sellars before she scrunched her nose in distaste. "You know I don't play well with others."

Sellars ignored the fuck you expression on Lacy's face. Right now she was in awe of her and Gabby's relationship. Maybe even jealous. It was adorable and fun. Unlike her own childhood. Her parents hadn't been loving or nurturing. They expected her and her siblings to draw the chalk line before they walked the straight and narrow path. To follow in their medical footsteps. To become doctors. Surgeons. To practice medicine in any capacity.

No deviations. No alternatives. And in the process, no hugs or kisses or tender moments. No encouraging words. They wanted their children to always behave. To always do as told. They wouldn't tolerate sibling rivalry or backyard wrestling. In other words, they weren't allowed to be kids. Wouldn't be caught dead playing in their Sunday best. They were to obey every command, at every moment. No wonder they shunned Sellars so much. She refused to obey anyone's commands except her own.

Until she fell in love with Sarah. Obeying her commands had been her pleasure.

As she stood back and watched Gabby and Lacy hug and tease as they walked toward the house, she couldn't help but feel like she'd missed out on something important. Lacy wasn't even blood to this family, yet she treated all of them like they were exactly that. Blood. The love was at surface level, blatant and carefree. The sight was moving, and it made her long for a childhood she could never have.

Would her life have turned out differently if she'd been allowed to stomp her foot? If she'd been allowed to have a feeling that showed on the outside? If they'd let her be herself, would she have been so hell-bent to do the opposite of what they said? Would she have considered becoming what they wanted if they'd just encouraged her? Was it that hard for a parent to be supportive of what their children wanted instead of the life they'd already instilled in them?

She would never know the answer. It had been almost five years since she'd spoken to her mother, and that phone call consisted of breaking the news that her sister had delivered baby number four. Her way of rubbing it in Sellars's face that she would never have children of her own.

It had been even more years since she'd seen her father. Sellars was okay with that. Her parents were better off without the black sheep anyway.

To stop the bad memories from digging too deep, Sellars followed the group inside, suddenly feeling like the fifth wheel and out of her element, a reaction she normally never experienced. Because for the first time, she *was* out of her element. Literally. This was Lacy's family. Billy was Lacy's best friend. Darlene and Gabby, all hers to love and cherish. Sellars was the outsider here. Always the outcast. Always on the outside looking in. She'd hardened herself to this reaction. Bricked herself against this emotion. Yet there it was once again, nudging at her anxiety, reminding her that even the mother that gave birth to her couldn't love her for the person she was.

"So, how much money do you owe the swear jar now that Daddy got to introduce you to Sellars?" Gabby asked, pulling herself up onto a stool at the kitchen counter. She tapped a mason jar with a pink ribbon wrapped around the lid, a tiny chalkboard on the face that read *My aunt has a potty mouth. Does yours?*

Before Lacy could answer, Gabby cut a sharp gaze to Sellars. "And in case you wondered, I most definitely noticed you didn't come home last night, which either means your car broke down, which is about as likely as a meteor landing on this house for as much as you work on it, or you got into trouble again, which is against the rules of your suspension."

Sellars opened her mouth to respond, but Gabby shushed her by snapping her index and thumb together.

"Aunt Lacy is here to set you straight if you haven't completely demolished your chance of ever racing again in the last few hours." Gabby narrowed her gaze, daring Sellars to say another word. "We'll discuss your nightly adventures later."

Billy snickered, and Sellars was positive heat was crawling across her cheeks. She'd never met a more opinionated child in her life. Or parents who allowed her to be herself, who loved her regardless of her blatant honesty.

If Lacy wasn't still hung up on the first sentence, she'd be proud of the little smart mouth Gabby. "What do you mean, came home? As in, here, right here, home?"

Gabby inched the swear jar in Lacy's direction. "Yes. Didn't Daddy tell you? Sellars is staying here while her apartment is being renovated."

Lacy cut a death glare on Billy. He turned away. "It appears your daddy has forgotten to tell me a lot."

"Since that little vein is popping out on the side of your neck." Gabby pushed the jar closer to Lacy. "I will have to require payment up front before you continue this conversation."

Lacy kept her gaze locked on Billy, wondering what he saw in Sellars that would make him so secretive. Normally, he wouldn't hide anything from her. Normally, all information was laid out on the table. The ball in her court, so to speak.

She wasn't a damsel. He never treated her as such. Yet right now, his refusal to make eye contact, said there was more to this story, a deeper reason he had taken a loser under his wing, why he'd moved her into his home.

Not that his reasons mattered. She wouldn't have any part of this scheme to fix the unfixable. Sellars was broken. Why, only Sellars knew. Why, Lacy didn't give a shit. But for sure, she wouldn't be participating.

"You may have to cut your aunt some slack on the fees, Miss Gabby." Sellars stepped beside Gabby and draped her arm across her shoulder. "She just turned down a babysitting job. A six-figure babysitting job. Five big ones, to be exact."

"She did?" Gabby's brow creased.

"She sure did." Sellars gave a firm nod.

Lacy cocked her head, freezing her poker face. Her heart somersaulted.

"Before you say another word," Gabby tapped the swear. jar harder, "I insist someone show me the money."

The fact that she'd just turned down a job that would pay her bills for life, or that could put her little project into motion, wasn't what rubbed her the wrong way.

It was Sellars's gesture that set Lacy on edge. That little "This is my buddy right here" gesture. Gabby was a smart kid. Smart-assed and extremely opinionated. The fact that she'd taken up with such a worthless human being didn't sit well in the pit of her stomach.

Not to mention that the sound five hundred thousand dollars made rolling off Sellars's tongue, had goose bumps threatening under her skin.

"I guess that means your aunt won't be able to buy herself a brand new attitude," Sellars added with a smirk.

Gabby's eyes widened and she thrust the jar toward Lacy. "I'm going to get so rich this month." She sucked her teeth together, slowly drew her cheeks back, and gave the signature Gabby smile.

Normally, that smile would be contagious. Normally, Lacy would burst into a laughing fit at how Gabby could break a mad spell with that corny smile. Not this time. Not with her mind replaying the dollar figure. Not with Sellars's arm draped around Gabby's shoulder like they were pals. As if Gabby could adore such a dimwit. And not with anger taking root. Not a fat fucking chance.

The laugh came out of Lacy's mouth before she knew it had formed.

"Gabby, you need to go upstairs!" Billy said, his sights locked on Lacy.

"Daddy! I'm about to earn enough money to buy all my Christmas presents in a single hour. I can't leave yet."

"Now, Gabby." He pointed toward the stairs.

Lacy continued to laugh, hearing the evil sound echoing back on her ears.

Gabby huffed and shoved the jar into Sellars's hands. "Make sure she pays up. Your Christmas present depends on it. Understand?" She dropped off the stool and hugged Lacy, which silenced the laughter even though the anger was still bubbling. "I love you past infinity, Aunt Lacy. But I expect money to be in that jar when I get up in the morning. We're going to spend the weekend with Grandma, and you know how much shopping she can do in a single day."

Gabby raced up the stairs while Lacy leveled her gaze on Sellars.

She started counting backward from ten, a lesson Gabby promised would solve some of Lacy's quick-tongued responses. As always, it was utter failure.

Ten...ni—

"Money can't buy a new fucking attitude anymore than it can buy you a goddamn conscious. You may have pulled the wool over that precious baby's eyes"—Lacy jabbed her finger toward the staircase where Gabby had just disappeared—"but you sure as fuck can't pull it over mine." Lacy took several steps toward Sellars, regretting the decision as soon as she saw that smirk transform into a heated smile. "And with the devil as my witness, if you even so much as put a fucking frown on her face, I will track you down like a rabid dog, yank that shit you call a head clean off your shoulders, and pull your blackened heart out through your *fucking* throat. Bank on that!"

Sellars's smile widened as she slowly pushed the swear jar toward Lacy. "I have no idea how much those f-bombs are worth, but I think you just bought us all Christmas presents."

"Fuck you."

"Okay, you two." Billy took a timid step toward them. "This isn't getting us anywhere."

Lacy tagged a death glare on him. "Oh, *now* you found your fucking tongue? Couldn't you have found it hours ago when you told me you had a little photography job for me?"

"That's no way to talk to your best friend." Sellars mockingly tapped the lid. "But Gabby will appreciate it."

Lacy jerked the jar from Sellars's grasp. "Don't you have somewhere else to be? Like back to hell where you came from?"

"I think hell is where you came from. Didn't you say the devil was your witness?" Sellars winked.

Lacy stepped forward, teeth grinding, unsure exactly why she was so pissed off or why she felt the need to lash out. So what if Sellars liked sabotaging her own career? So what if she liked stirring the pot with the other racers because she couldn't keep her dick in her pants? What did it matter to Lacy what Sellars did with her life?

Because she'd made a little girl, her little girl, her Gabby, her little smart-ass twin, adore her. That's why. And she was mad at Billy for allowing it. Inviting it.

Billy stepped forward and defensively held up his hands. "Stop. Both of you. Just stop!"

"Little late for that, wouldn't you say?" Lacy backed a step away from Sellars, hating that she liked the way Sellars smelled.

She had a musky scent to her. And she smelled like gasoline. She reminded Lacy of a past she could never have again. Being in the pit with the race car drivers and their crews. The aroma of oil and fuel all around her. Snapping their pics and adoring their fun banter. She missed those days. Missed being able to support Billy.

Now, all she could do was sneak a few paragraphs from the tabloids in a grocery store checkout line, grab a few minutes of the news, before those horrible images of death snaked their way inside.

Why did she have to be the one? The one to capture someone's death. Doug's death, of all people? To be accused of selling those photos to the highest bidder, as if she could ever stoop so low.

She'd loved that man. Adored his wife and children.

"I think you need to hear her out, Lacy," Billy said, yanking Lacy out of the memories.

"I don't need to hear a single word to know this bitch is a worthless cause." Lacy swung her gaze back on Sellars. "We both know no dollar amount will fix her. Her career crashed and burned in a fucking smoke-filled nightclub with another racer's wife on the tip of that tongue."

Sellars offered a smile that sent heat gathering between Lacy's thighs. "You know, I'm standing right here. You don't have to say *her* like I can't hear you." She cocked her head and gave a wink. "And don't fret, sexy. There's enough of me to go around if that's what you're worried about."

"Over my dead, goddamn body."

Sellars winked again and Lacy resisted rushing at her. She'd never disliked someone so much in her life. Dislike that was running a dangerous parallel path alongside twisted need.

Her crotch was a wet mess while her mind was screaming obscenities.

"Sellars, can you please just explain it to her?" Billy pleaded.

Lacy crossed her arms. Truth was, she wanted to hear this answer. She needed to know who thought Sellars was worth five hundred grand. Someone wanted to save her and was willing to pay a pretty penny to see that she didn't self-destruct. The answer should be interesting. Also, if she was going to be honest with herself, she needed that money. That chunk of cash would help her quit the dead-end career she'd shoved herself into, would give her the funds to pack up and move to Pittsburgh where she knew she belonged, and put her close to this beloved family.

"Please. Waste some more of my time." Lacy arched a brow.

"Okay. My sponsor wants to pay you to follow me around to events, snap some bullcrap photos, and then tag them to social media in hopes of revamping my fan base."

"Pfft. As if you ever had a fan base."

"Lacy," Billy warned her.

Sellars shrugged. "What can I say? Some people like my drama."

"So what's the catch?" Lacy looked between them. "You're not worth that kind of money. Especially since your dumbass has already nosedived tonight. Didn't we pick you up from jail?"

Sellars looked away. "I'm sure my sponsor will take care of it. He always does."

Lacy cut her gaze to Billy who shook his head, warning her once again. Sucked that she couldn't be warned out of bad behavior either.

"So no accountability for your actions. That explains a lot."

"To save from more arguing," Billy said, "why don't you go with Sellars to the sponsor meeting in the morning and then make a decision."

"I don't see the point, but sure. I have some old friends to visit in town anyway." Lacy grabbed her bag and took a step toward the stairs.

"Wrong way, sexy." Sellars walked around her. "The spare room is mine for now."

Lacy swung around to stare at Billy who looked like someone trapped in the headlight of an oncoming train. "You're going to stick me in the man cave? Why can't you stick her ass down there so she can come and go with her trashy sluts at will?"

"Speaking of trashy. Are those your dental floss thongs in the dresser?" Sellars took in a deliberate deep breath, then she winked and started up the stairs. "See you at sunrise, ice princess."

Once again, Lacy was left to fume. She turned a shocked glare on Billy.

"Kip Sellars? The spiraling out of control, fuck everything on two legs, famous street racing thug, NASCAR rookie everyone loves to hate because she likes their wives, a lot? Think you could have given me a heads-up?"

Billy gave her that pitiful frown that used to melt girls' hearts, then shrugged. "I love you."

"Screw you." Lacy snatched the handle of her luggage and headed for the basement.

"I *love* you!" Billy blurted.

Lacy flipped him a bird over her shoulder. "Sit and spin, assface."

"You love me and you know it," Billy said as she reached the basement door.

"Of course I do. It's the only reason you're still breathing." Lacy turned the handle of the basement door.

"You'll take the job, won't you?" Billy asked before she started down the steps.

"Of course I'll take the job. How else will I buy myself a new attitude?"

Lacy heard the loud clap of his hand as she slammed the door behind her.

CHAPTER FIVE

Lacy stepped out of the man cave and found the great room and kitchen empty. Perfect. She needed coffee before she had to face Sellars once again. Before she had to endure that delicious spice one more time. Before she had to endure that "you have met your match" smirk that seemed to be a permanent expression on Sellars's face.

Fact was, she hadn't met too many people who could take her, let alone match her. And positively none had ever attempted to one-up her. Sellars was proving she wasn't going to lie down and allow Lacy to walk all over her, although walking on her wasn't quite what she'd envisioned half the night in her fitful sleep.

She admired that about Sellars. That she wouldn't let anyone get the upper hand. Though that trait wasn't going to make Lacy play nice. Not even the notion of being paid handsomely would make her alter her extreme dislike for Kip Sellars.

But the money sure would make her tolerate just a little bit more. She'd tossed and turned all night, dollar figures and plans and the possibility of a new beginning that would bloom from this paycheck, dancing in her mind. Excitement had overruled her need for sleep.

To take that excitement to another level, she'd started texting Patrick, her best gay friend on the opposite side of the map, at two in the morning to vent about Sellars and to tell him that their pet project could possibly be taken to another level if everything fell into place. That is, if she didn't kill Sellars first.

She'd met Patrick at one of the many homeless shelters in LA and soon learned that they shared the same interest in the homeless. In their well-being. Of making sure they got a hot meal several times a week. They visited the shelters often to just hang out, talk to them, to treat them like they weren't walking the streets looking for a handout because something in their life had knocked them to their knees. Her passion for photography had quickly come into play, starting by capturing them in their surroundings, later by letting them be the photographer by taking the disposable cameras she and Patrick provided to those interested.

She'd been shocked at what they brought back, what she and Patrick developed. The heart, the center of their world. Their hiding spots. Their raw, unfiltered lives. The lives that no one could ever imagine. Beneath bridges, in abandoned buildings, in makeshift houses constructed of cardboard, sometimes tents or tarps, they were hidden in plain sight.

Lacy and Patrick had been so moved, so in awe of their pictures, they'd handed out more cameras. She even paid them for their troubles and now, two years later, they had photo albums full, more framed in their homes, with so many more she would love to show the world.

The money to babysit a misfit could make the project happen. Those remarkable photos could adorn art galleries across the world, drawing in the funds needed to broaden the plans. This project could go global. Could help so many who truly wanted to make a change, who couldn't seem to catch a break.

With a mug of coffee in her hand, Lacy pulled herself onto a stool, determined to play nice today. If she had to bite her tongue to get that money, she would find a way.

Actually, that had been Patrick's demand. For Lacy to play nice. Which he knew was a job all by itself.

Something caught her attention, and she turned to find a white sock dancing around the wall of the stairs, spinning like a Terrible Towel at a Steelers football game.

She couldn't help but smile at Billy's silly call for a truce. God, how she loved that man.

"There better be diamond earrings in that sock if you want to be forgiven this soon."

Billy stuck his head around the wall. "You hate diamonds and all things that glitter."

"Yeah. True." She gave him a wink of forgiveness.

He descended the stairs at the same time the front door opened and Sellars stepped inside. Lacy's anger spiked for a split second and then slowly turned to that unfamiliar emotion of hatred and balled up need as she took in Sellars's sweaty face and neck, black smudge marks on her cheeks and hands, and dressed in a pair of ripped jeans and too tight T-shirt. Her hair was a dark, sexy mess. No wonder mature women with name-branded husbands had been unable to turn down such a delicious invitation.

Footsteps vibrated down the stairs, and two seconds later, Gabby vaulted over the bottom rail. "Neither of you are allowed to speak to each other until you pay the swear jar!" She looked between them, jar out like a homeless person's cup. "My shopping trip is paid for after last night's blowout. Thank you, Aunt Lacy. So today I'll work on a complete new wardrobe. Mine is getting a little out of style," she ended with a grin.

Lacy couldn't take her eyes off Sellars. The fact that she was so turned on twisted her mood even more sour. There wasn't a single thing she wanted to admire about this train wreck. Not even that tight body. Or that slick skin. Or those lean legs. Or the six-pack detailed through the fabric of her shirt.

Nothing. Not a fucking thing. But damn if she could spread the emotions apart.

"Give me ten minutes to shower off this grunge and we'll be on our way." Sellars darted up the stairs.

"That's it?" Gabby asked. "Did you guys kiss and make up after I went to bed?" She thrust the jar out to Lacy.

Lacy dug in the pocket of her jeans and withdrew a twenty. She folded it and shoved it into the slot of the lid. "Not a fat fucking chance in hell, you beautiful soul, you."

"Whew. Thought I was going to have to dip into my savings." Gabby strolled into the kitchen and pulled a box of cereal out of the cabinet.

Fifteen minutes later, Sellars emerged looking far more edible than Lacy needed. From her black Converse shoes and faded blue jeans to the charcoal blazer over a black T-shirt, she was slick as glass. Lacy reminded herself that the weekend was coming. Everyone would be gone to visit Grandma, and she could spend some time trolling the nightclubs. A quick fuck might be just what the doctor ordered with so much hostility, and eye candy, floating around.

"You ready?" Sellars dangled the keys. "My car was delivered this morning from the impound lot."

"Let me guess." Lacy took a long sip of her coffee, trying to breathe back the triggered hot flash, hating that her insides were clamped tight, and set the mug on the counter. She slid off the stool to stare up into those eyes. "Some kind of slick muscle car." With a casual inspection, she let her gaze drop down Sellars's body. Her insides tightened again. "No doubt, a classic pony, likely a Camaro, some old sleek super sport, probably a convertible, because a piece of—"

"Swear jar!" Gabby said.

Without looking away, Lacy dug into her pants pocket and pulled out another bill. She tossed it onto the counter and stuck her hand back into the pocket.

"—shit like you thinks a car is nothing more than a pussy magnet. An egotistical dickweed like you would drive nothing other than something that would draw all the attention her way." Lacy withdrew another bill and slapped it on the counter, her anger notching as Sellars's brow arched with humor. "So let's get one thing straight, fuckface. Cars don't turn me on." She took another step toward Sellars, dug another bill out of her pocket, and tossed it with the others. "And women who drive them, disgust the ever loving need to fuck right out of me."

Sellars looked over at Billy, then slowly cut her sights to Gabby before landing looking back to Lacy. "In Pittsburgh, when someone dangles the keys, it means they're offering to be the chauffeur. Sorry if you confused the shiny round metal for a proposal," she bent down and whispered, "there's only one reason I get on bended knee." She winked, then turned and started for the front door. "I'll be in the car waiting."

Lacy watched her stroll across the room, her insides a slick mess. God, it was hot to have someone fight back with her, to not let her have the upper hand. Sucked for Sellars that till her dying breath, Lacy would always have the last word. Or die trying.

She dug in her pocket, blew Gabby a kiss, fished out the remaining bills she had in her pocket, and tossed them on the counter. "Paid in advance. It's gonna be a long day."

Fifteen minutes later, Lacy was regretting the decision to ride with Sellars in her restored '69 convertible Camaro. The thing moved with grace. Not a single rattle. Now she knew what Gabby had meant when she said there was a slim chance the car had broken down. Sellars probably spent every spare minute tinkering beneath the hood. Just like this morning.

And Lord help her, she looked damn good driving it. Her hand cupping the gearshift, blazer sleeves rolled up, showing the muscles in her lower arm. Her leg lifting against the clutch made her thighs tighten. Her smooth ease moving with the traffic.

There was only one flaw. She drove like a fucking grandma. Obeying every speed limit. Lacy hadn't expected that. She was a racer, after all. She had expected a little wind in her hair, trading lanes to move around slower traffic. Hell, she'd wanted that. Deep down, she'd wanted the speed. Wanted a little of that adrenaline she missed so much by watching the racers on the track.

When they finally pulled alongside the Wyndham Grand Hotel, Lacy breathed a sigh of relief. "Think you could have gotten us here any slower?" She opened the door and got out at the same time the valet crossed in front of the car.

Sellars tossed the man the keys. "Usual spot, Phillip?"

"You bet." He ducked into the seat and revved the engine with a smile, then pulled into the garage.

Lacy heard the faint echo as it appeared to climb.

Sellars walked past her. "Sorry. I only do warp speed when there's a challenge involved. You, my dear, are no challenge at all." She kept walking into the building, leaving Lacy no choice but to follow and fume until they came to the elevator doors.

"Last chance to back out," Sellars said.

"Without meeting the person who thinks you actually still have a chance at a future?" Lacy cocked her head. "Not a chance in hell."

The elevator door opened, and they stepped inside. "You seem obsessed with hell. Did you leave all of your friends there while on vacation?"

The door closed while Lacy grinned. "I don't have friends."

"I believe that." Sellars watched the panel tick off the number of floors.

Before Lacy could respond, the elevator stopped on the top floor and opened to reveal Mr. Reynolds. His hair was completely silver, unlike the last time Lacy had seen him around the track. Had it been that long? Seemed like only yesterday she had the race car in her zoom lens seconds before a death.

She swallowed hard as a smile lit his face and he extended his hand. "Great to see you again, Lacy. How have you been?"

Lacy offered a bittersweet nod. "Life is great, Mr. Reynolds. I can't complain." She lied. She complained every day of her life. Sometimes every minute of every hour she was cursed to shoot a bridezilla having a meltdown.

"Great to hear. Come have a seat." He clapped Sellars on the back then led the way to a large rectangular table by the windows that overlooked the Point.

Heinz Field emerged like a gentle giant across the river, and Lacy reminded herself she needed to hit the Strip District before her vacation was over. She needed the latest memorabilia to take back home, specifically something for Patrick, who she had finally turned into a fan with her constant affection for the Steelers.

Mr. Reynolds was no more in his seat before he turned a scolding eye on Sellars and slapped his hand on the table.

So much for stalling business. "Arrested again? Are you deliberately trying to get kicked out of NASCAR? Out of racing? What more can I do to save your ass, Kip?" He threw his hands to the side before driving forward. "How many more times do I have to save your ass before you give me no choice but to throw in the towel?"

Lacy turned to look at Sellars, liking Mr. Reynolds already.

Sellars simply shrugged, her gaze trained on the window. "It's just money. Isn't that right? Isn't that what you've always said, Granddaddy?" She finally turned to look at him, her expression blank. "Isn't that how you make all problems in life go away? Just toss a little money at it?"

Lacy cocked a brow. Grandfather? The sponsor, Mr. Reynolds, was her grandfather?

Holy hell. That explained a lot. Sellars was a silver spoon baby. No doubt she was catered to her entire life. Probably never had a spanking or had to pick her own hickory switch.

Dear Lord, she was dealing with a spoiled rich brat who thought she could lure pussy to her car with a simple rev of that sweet engine.

Mr. Reynolds quickly looked at Lacy then slowly back to Sellars. He leaned back in his chair with a grunt. "Back to that. Always back to that."

Sellars stared at him for several seconds before she tagged her sights back on the window.

Mr. Reynolds looked over at Lacy again. "Did she explain anything to you? What I'm willing to pay you to keep her out of trouble for three more weeks?"

Lacy shuffled a glance between them. "Well, not really. What exactly is it that you need me to do?"

He tapped a finger on the desk. "I've taken the liberty of signing her up for a few events. Fundraisers, community outings, so to speak." He looked down at his hands for a second. "She needs to get her face back in the spotlight." He shot Sellars a glare. "The good spotlight. Not these immature tantrums she's been putting on for show."

Sellars ground her teeth. "Tantrums? Who—"

Lacy cleared her throat and interrupted. "So you just need me to photograph her during the events?"

"I need you to keep her out of trouble." He glanced back to Sellars who was still staring out that window. "She can't seem to do it on her own."

"Pardon my confusion, Mr. Reynolds. I feel like I'm missing the punch line. A few photo shoots doesn't seem rational for the price you're offering."

"There's no punch line." He leaned against the table. "I need someone with the photo skills, who knows the ins and outs of social media, and can keep her in check until NASCAR lifts her suspension."

"You want me to babysit a grown woman who seems hell-bent on doing whatever she wants?" Lacy asked. "How do I fit into this picture? I'm not a kindergarten teacher."

He smiled. "You're a pretty girl, Lacy. She likes pretty girls. I'm sure you'll figure something out."

Sellars shot out of the chair so fast, it tipped over with a loud bang. "Jesus! You just don't know when to stop, do you?"

She barged across the room, stepped into the elevator, expecting Lacy to be behind her, running from a crude insinuation.

When she turned to see Lacy was still sitting in the chair, eyes wide, lips parted, anger ripped through her. She slammed her finger on the down button and moved back until the doors closed.

Just like everyone else in her life. Lacy was going to be easily bought. Just like Sarah's grandmother. Sarah had been killed at the hands of Sellars. An accident, mind you, but she, too, had been bought. No police were involved. No jail for Sellars. Not even a smack on the wrist for the empty liquor bottles in the car. Nothing. Not a damn thing had happened except silence. Radio silence.

She hadn't been invited to the funeral. The remaining family had opted for a private burial. One Sellars wasn't welcome to attend.

Gone. Sarah was just gone. Riding shotgun beside her one minute, the next, gone.

Months later, she heard the rumor that Sarah's grandmother had sold her house and moved. Likely, to some lavish resort where she would live out the rest of her days surrounded by blue, sparkling water.

Seemed only Sellars had been cursed to carry the guilt around for the rest of her life while everyone else continued on as if someone hadn't died.

Someone had died. The love of her life had been killed. Sellars had killed her. And in everyone's rush to put all the pieces back together, to right the wrongs, they'd forgotten Sellars was shattered and broken and lost.

Nothing had ever been the same. Nothing ever would be again.

Lacy watched the doors swoosh closed before she turned to stare at Mr. Reynolds. She scooted to the edge of her chair, anger bubbling hard and fast. "Mr. Reynolds, I'm not exactly sure what you're trying to insinuate, but let me clarify my job description. I'm not a damn babysitter nor am I a fucking escort. You can't control me with your bank account. Am I clear?"

"I'm willing to pay you five hundred thousand dollars to keep her out of trouble. Just three weeks, Miss McGowen. That's all I need." He looked away and Lacy could read the desperation in his expression.

She had no idea what was going on in this family, was positive she didn't want to know, but she wasn't for sale and didn't appreciate that he assumed she was.

"I'm a photographer, Mr. Reynolds. Not a hooker." Lacy leaned back in her chair and took in a calming breath. "Never make the mistake of suggesting otherwise ever again."

His gaze went to the window. "I apologize. I just don't know what to do anymore. It's like she's still punishing me. I just wanted to save her. To make it go away."

Lacy remained quiet when all she really wanted to do was push out of her own chair and escape via the same route Sellars had.

As if he'd read her mind, he turned clear eyes on her. "I'll throw in exclusive photographer rights to all of my racing teams if you can pull this off. I need her to make it to the starting line, Lacy. Her skill will take her from there."

Lacy almost laughed, and cried. Once again, Mr. Reynolds was showing his true, uncaring colors. But in the same breath, he'd shown how much he truly loved his granddaughter.

With a smile, Lacy pushed the chair away from the table. "I'm going to assume that dementia has made you forget my past, the very past that made me leave NASCAR and this city to begin with. How dare you think that I would want to walk back into the same life with assholes just like you who use bully tactics to get what they want."

Mr. Reynolds held his hand out. "No. No! That's not what I meant. I didn't mean, I just…" He shook his head. "Once again, I am sorry. I never meant to upset you. Please sit down."

Lacy stood her ground. "Your bedside manner is disturbing, Mr. Reynolds. So let me save us both the trouble and let you know how I can be persuaded to babysit your otherwise reckless granddaughter."

❖

For the next thirty minutes, Sellars paced the sidewalk, wishing she hadn't left Lacy to deal with her grandfather, knowing Lacy would exit with a fat bank account, just like everyone else in her life it seemed.

Why were people so easily bought? How could they sell themselves so short? Did money really rule?

The doors swished open and Lacy stepped out.

Sellars couldn't help the growl that rumbled through her chest. "So, how much were you worth? The whole five hundred thousand? Or did you purse those lips, bat those sweet chocolate eyes, and sweet-talk him into doubling his offer?"

Lacy cocked a brow and Sellars resisted the urge to step into her, to bend down and capture those lips before hellfire escaped them. "I don't think we've been properly introduced, shitface. So let me get you up to speed." She stepped toward Sellars and inhaled the scent of her. "I'm worth far more than you'll ever earn in your fucking lifetime. And all the riches in the world couldn't force me to sell out. Not even to save my own soul. That, oh twisted one, is your domain." She took in a short breath and stepped closer. "Like you, I never get on my knees for anything, or anyone, but I won't hesitate to push a bitch down on hers."

Sellars stared down into those angry eyes and saw lust dancing in them.

"Now that we've been properly introduced, I'm going to leave you to stew in your own family drama. I have a friend waiting for me across the street." She glanced toward the blinking walk sign on the pole, pushed around Sellars, and started across the road.

Sellars watched her walk away, her insides clenching, her mind overflowing dangerously fast at the very image of dropping to her knees, making a feast out of that little fireball, or better, forcing Lacy down on hers.

Lacy called out to a man who was holding a "Need food. Please help" sign whose smile showed his adoration as Lacy got closer and waved in return. When Lacy made it to the sidewalk, she hugged him like a long lost friend.

Sellars hesitantly followed, curious about the interaction. She'd been taught to stay clear of the homeless with their little paper cups and signs that begged for help of any sort. Don't make eye contact; her parents had engraved that message on her soul. So she hadn't. She'd noticed them, of course, but kept walking, ignoring their pleas for even the simple change in her pocket.

She had a sneaky suspicion that Lacy was going to show her what a stuck-up snob she'd been all her life.

CHAPTER SIX

L acy and Sellars made their way back to the hotel after spending over an hour with Ralph.

Sellars learned a hell of a lot about Lacy in that little time. That she cared deeply for the homeless men and women in this city. That she knew almost all of them by name, their stories, and that she must be spending a tiny fortune sending money to the local McDonald's to feed any of them who stepped inside for food.

It was an eye-opener, actually. She didn't want to like Lacy, but who could hate a person who thought so much of those less fortunate? Lacy was all about the underdog, it seemed.

It was hot, actually. She'd never met anyone who put others above themselves. Not even her own parents.

"We need to head to the opposite side of town. We have an appointment," Lacy said as she stepped into the crosswalk, wondering why Sellars had been so quiet for the past hour.

Was it Ralph? The homeless man. With Sellars's background of rich parents, a filthy rich grandfather, she'd likely never been that close to one. Let alone had lunch with one.

She had a little over an hour to get Sellars to the fashion designer. Mr. Reynolds expected her to be freshly cut and newly attired for the upcoming gala event. An event Lacy wasn't too thrilled about attending herself. She didn't like stuffy surroundings, especially when those surroundings would be filled with snooty rich people, all putting on their best behavior for the sake of their careers.

Fake. Everyone would likely be fake.

But if she was going to get what she wanted, a full-blown art gallery event displaying all of those photographs for all the homeless who relied on handouts and good-hearted people, she was forced to play by his rules. If he wanted Sellars dressed to the nines for the event, then come hell or high water, that's exactly how Lacy would deliver her.

"How did you get involved with the homeless?" Sellars asked.

Lacy walked a little faster, wishing she could outrun her past as easily as it was to pull away from Sellars. The answer was a direct link to that past.

"Self-medicating myself," Lacy answered as they stepped onto the curb outside the hotel.

She wouldn't include that it had been her mother's idea to help her get over the ugly death she'd witnessed or all of the backlash and media that came after. Lacy had been in a bad place mentally after the fatal wreck. She'd already packed her bags and left Pittsburgh, LA bound, to get far away from anything and everything that had to do with racing. Months later, she still couldn't close her eyes without seeing the images. Those horrible images that had changed her life forever.

Her mom suggested using her camera, the very camera she couldn't look at without crying, and start slow. To capture the world around her. A bird in flight. A turtle in a creek. Fish in a pond. Slow moving nature, she'd said.

Finally, Lacy bit the bullet and hesitantly picked up the camera, feeling its weight and the power it truly held. The power to capture death. To freeze that death forever. And as hard as it was to hold it after so much time, those long walks she'd forced herself to endure through her neighborhood, eventually through the city, had been more therapeutic than she ever thought possible.

Things in LA were different from the greenery she'd always been surrounded by in West Virginia, her home state, or even Pittsburgh where traffic could come to a crawl quickly during rush hour. Concrete replaced plush grass. Car horns replaced the chirp of crickets and croak of tree frogs at night. Yet she'd found the most beautiful piece of life on those crowded streets. The homeless.

They were hidden in plain sight, camouflaged by the bustle of everyday life passing them by, but she'd found their beauty. They stood still in the chaos. They were frozen in time while the world swiftly moved around them. Lacy saw them. Their worn down expressions. Their heavy heads. Their rough features.

From afar, she'd captured them. Their signs that begged for a handout. Their interactions with each other. The way people didn't notice them at all, no matter what the heartfelt words were on their cardboard signs. Their pleas were condensed to a few simple words with a magic marker.

They just simply wanted to live.

Each day she returned, eventually with food and drinks. Sometimes with cigarettes. Sometimes with only her camera. Soon, she became a familiar face. They opened up to her. They told her about their lives now, as well as the lives that led them to the streets to begin with.

Some had been runaways, choosing that life over the ones they'd fled. Others had hit rock bottom either in the form of drugs, maybe financially. Regardless of the path that had led them to this place and time, they were family to each other, and their compassion for each other stood out like a diamond while business suits snubbed their noses, while people barked at someone who accidentally bumped into them, while women dropped their folders of papers and no one stopped to assist. They helped each other. Gave up their food for those less fortunate in the day's hunt. Even gave up their makeshift houses for newbies who were scared and frightened of this new world they'd fallen victim to.

Soon, Lacy was a constant face in their lives. They brightened when they saw her. Accepted the disposable cameras she offered. Smiled when she brought them the developed photos, bragging about their talent.

"You self-medicate by feeding the homeless? Wouldn't an Ativan do the trick?"

"Sure, if I wanted to become a prescription junkie." They rounded the corner of the hotel and Sellars motioned to the valet that she was ready for her car. "I believe alcohol and sleazy sluts is your choice of medicine?"

Sellars shot her a look. "Jealous?"

Lacy grinned. "Only of everyone else around me at this exact moment in time, for they are lucky to not be standing here beside you."

"You never answered my question." Sellars stuffed her hands in her pockets. "How much were you worth, Lacy?"

Lacy took in the calm way she'd asked the question. Someone in her life, someone she cared about, had sold out to her grandfather. Who? Why?

She lifted her chin at the same time Sellars's car pulled out of the garage. "Your grandfather can't afford me. Neither can you."

The car came to a stop beside them, and the valet got out, leaving the door open. He dangled the keys.

Lacy quickly plucked them from his grasp. "Oh, look. A shiny proposal. I do believe I accept the offer." She ducked into the driver's seat and closed the door.

Sellars stood on the sidewalk, her jaw clenched.

Lacy cranked the car and revved the engine. Holy damn, but she could feel the power beneath her. The energy felt good, and she revved again simply to feel the vibration running through her. Is this what a real race car felt like? Sure, she'd been close to them, but not once had she been inside one. As much as Billy had encouraged her in the past, before she was too terrified to get near a track, but she'd always chosen to watch from afar.

Sellars yanked open the passenger door and dropped into the seat. "One scratch, there will be hell to pay."

Lacy pushed the shifter into drive. "It's just money, right?" Without waiting for Sellars's response, Lacy pulled away from the curb, checked for traffic, and darted out, inhaling the adrenaline.

She missed racing. Being close to the action. Missed being in the pit with the roar of those engines circling her.

But most of all, she missed being a part of Billy's world. His passion. Racing was his life. He loved it so much. Yet Lacy couldn't force herself to overcome the anxiety the track forced upon her.

Even for him, she couldn't do it.

Lacy circled back through the city, secretly wishing she was among the crowd walking along the shops, and made her way onto the freeway where she pushed the pedal a little harder and smiled at how the car obeyed instantly.

"Are we late for a date?" Sellars asked, but Lacy could hear the approval in her voice. "Speaking of, where are we going?"

"I scored you a fitting with a designer. A personal friend of mine."

"A fitting? Like a clothes designer? I don't think so."

"You dodge death for a living." Lacy glanced at her. "Surely you're not afraid of the latest fashions." Sellars's arched brow was too sexy so Lacy turned back to look at the open road. "Besides, you have an event scheduled for tomorrow night that I am forced to chaperone because your fucking ass doesn't know how to act your age."

"Never had any complaints about my maturity."

Lacy could feel those eyes staring at her and refused to look over. "Fully describes the company you keep. I'm sure they're just as mature."

"I'll pass on my grandfather's need to show himself off to the whole world by nicknaming it a get-together."

"You will not pass. This isn't some game that you get to choose to play or pass, dumbass. You got yourself into this mess and you'll fucking do what he says."

"What is your beef with me?"

"The truth, or do you want the 'hurt your feelings' version?" Lacy merged around a slow car before she dared make eye contact.

Sellars had beautiful eyes. Sexy, deep green eyes.

"I don't have feelings," Sellars said.

Lacy giggled. "Bullshit. You flew out of your grandfather's office like a fucking scorned toddler. So yes, Miss Terrible Two, you have feelings."

Sellars inhaled and blew the breath out slowly but didn't respond.

"Sorry to have misled you in my previous statement. Both versions, truth and otherwise, equate to the same ending of hurt feelings." Lacy moved back into the slow lane. "I think you are dog shit, who cares about no one but yourself, who won't have a career at the end of this little babysitting job, and you'll blame every living creature but yourself because that's what self-centered, silver spoon fed infants grow up to be. Self-centered, adult version pricks."

"Wow. I never knew you thought so highly of me." Sellars moved her attention back to the windshield.

Lacy wished she could feel bad, but she couldn't. She didn't like Sellars, didn't like her personality, or the way she chose to flaunt it, even if she was hot as sin. If it wasn't for the future of the homeless everywhere, a possible link to endless funding for their well-being, she would have never picked up the white towel in the first place. She could have told Mr. Reynolds where to shove his inconsiderate demeanor. However, she had a good grip on that white towel and was waving it like a fan at a Steelers game. All she had to do was throw it down and the game was all over. She was in control as long as she could keep Sellars in check.

Question was, how the hell was she going to pull that off when Sellars had a path of her own she seemed hell-bent to stay on?

The rest of the drive was spent in silence, and as soon as Lacy killed the engine, Sellars jerked the keys from the ignition and shoved out of the car.

Lacy led the way inside the building and found Aggie— Agnes to those who weren't on a personal level with her— smiling at her from across the room. And personal, they were.

She'd met Aggie at one of the local nightclubs while visiting Billy. She was surrounded by a group of ogling admirers. At the time, Lacy had no clue who she was. Didn't care what her status or career was. The only thing she cared about was being trapped in those brown, flirty eyes and needing to take her up on the non-verbal offer.

An hour later, Lacy had landed on her back in the middle of Aggie's king-size bed, naked, ready.

She'd run into her again the next year. On purpose, of course. But the third year, Aggie had been snatched out of the sea of available bachelorettes by a pretty little blonde who seemed to think the sun rose and set on Aggie's head. They were cute together, and Lacy had hugged her and wished her well before she went in search of fresh meat.

The sun never rose or set on anyone's head in Lacy's world. All she wanted to rise were her hips with someone sitting between them.

And here she was again, in Aggie's presence, not feeling the least bit of emotion.

"My beautiful, sexy Lacy," Aggie purred as she made her way across the room. She wrapped her arms around Lacy, hands cupping her ass, completely ignoring Sellars, and she lifted her off the floor in a tight hug. "Oh, how I have missed the scent and the feel and the look of you."

Lacy hugged her back. "I missed you too, Aggie." She wiggled out of the fondling embrace and nodded toward Sellars. "Here she is. Kip Sellars in the flesh."

Sellars frowned at the statement, but mainly she was still frazzled by Aggie's touchy-feely hug, her hands gripping Lacy's ass like it had many times before. For sure, they had before.

She wasn't sure why that bothered her so much.

Aggie turned her attention toward Sellars and began a slow circle around her. "Nice, tight ass. Great build. I have many delicious ideas for you." She continued the walkabout before coming to a stop in front of her again. "Gives me great pleasure to know you haven't tasted this little tangy dessert. Yet."

Aggie cut her gaze back on Lacy and winked. "Are you free tonight? I haven't had you in years."

Sellars cocked a brow and resisted taking Lacy by the hand and leading her out of this woman's presence. Something about her was rubbing Sellars the wrong way.

"Not tonight, bad girl. I have to babysit this misfit," Lacy said before she poked a finger into Aggie's broad chest. "And stop misbehaving. Cheryl would cut your balls off."

Aggie laughed, and Sellars relaxed at the notion that this woman was taken. Not that it meant very much. But at the least, it would make her think twice about cheating.

Sellars didn't like cheaters. Sure, she'd screwed cheaters, unknowingly, but didn't think she could ever be the cheater. It was too easy to break up and walk away if the love was absent. Cheating was a piss ant excuse to use for a breakup.

Aggie suddenly stopped laughing. She stepped into Lacy, grabbed her around the waist with one arm, and tugged Lacy against her chest. "Give me the word, you delectable piece of heaven, and I'll twist my own balls off with a set of needle-nose pliers and gift wrap them for her."

"You're such a bullshitter. Cheryl is your complete other half." Lacy nodded toward Sellars. "Now go get your ass to work transforming this reckless newbie."

Aggie loosed her grip on Lacy and turned to Sellars. "Let's go find you something worthy of being this beautiful creature's escort."

An hour later, Lacy could feel Sellars losing her patience. Every new outfit was worse than the first. Not worse, as everything Aggie designed was tasteful and stylish. But it wasn't perfect for Sellars. Actually, she'd been perfect walking through the door.

Not too many people could pull off the blue jean, T-shirt, and blazer look, but Sellars wore it with perfection. Truthfully, she didn't need a new wardrobe. She was excellent exactly as she was. However, Mr. Reynolds had stipulated the importance of her attire for the gala, and no matter what Lacy thought, he had the checkbook.

Nearby was a rack of costumes. Lacy went to inspect and found a pair of Elton John sunglasses, a black top hat, and a boa. She donned them, grabbed her camera, and snuck up behind Sellars as Aggie inspected her in the floor length mirror, insisting the ensemble would be perfect for the lavish gala.

Lacy rose over Sellars's shoulder, made a silly face in the mirror, and snapped the picture just as Sellars narrowed her brow. She rose again at a different angle, gave a shocked expression, and snapped another picture. Once again, she gave a different expression and snapped, until Sellars loosened her tight jawline. Lacy stuck her ass out to one side of Sellars, watching the reflection, then pursed her lips and once again, snapped the photo. She continued making silly poses until Sellars cracked a smile and joined in the fun by altering her own poses.

Besides the sarcastic smirks, Lacy was positive this was the first time she'd seen Sellars smile. A real smile. She was a hard woman. A hardness Lacy had no desire to soften. But she was curious what kind of rift caused the gap between her and her grandfather, especially considering he was the money behind the speed. The only thing keeping Sellars afloat in her otherwise sinking ship.

Something bad, for sure. But again, Lacy had no desire to dig for the root. It was family drama she wanted no part of.

After another wardrobe change and more crazy poses, Lacy saw this adventure was useless. Sellars was being a good sport, but Lacy could tell she was a ticking time bomb.

To hell with her grandfather. If he had a problem with Sellars's clothing, he would surely get over it.

He had more fish to fry, anyway. Like holding his breath until NASCAR lifted her suspension.

"Aggie, we will have to get back with you on her choices. We have another pressing appointment we need to get to." Lacy lied and watched the relief crawl across Sellars's face.

Fact was, she planned on locking herself in the basement to go through the photos she'd taken before she started winging a select few into cyberspace. She could only cross her fingers that she would make a dent in Sellars's hateful fan base. If that was even possible this late in the race.

"I need to show you a design I think would look spectacular on you for the gala." Aggie took a step toward Lacy. "Alone."

Lacy chuckled. "I didn't come equipped with a ball gown, and I trust you. So I'll take it."

"Aren't you curious to see the design first?" Aggie arched a pleading brow.

"And take away the element of surprise? Absolutely not."

"Won't you at least allow me the pleasure of seeing you in it? And then out of it?" Aggie pursed her lips.

Lacy wagged her finger. "Your true colors are oozing out again. And we really do have to run."

Aggie swung her gaze on Sellars.

Sellars gave her a firm nod, playing along with the lie.

Aggie stepped into Lacy and placed her hands around the curve of Lacy's hips. "I'll send a courier to Billy's with your dress first thing in the morning. But next time, you come alone. I beg you."

A knot tightened in Sellars's stomach as Aggie leaned down and pressed her lips against Lacy's. It was a quick show of affection, but the look in her eyes said there was so much more being offered.

"Behave yourself before I have to tattletale on you." Lacy winked.

"That's impossible. I can't behave around you." Aggie stepped back and let her gaze slide down Lacy's body. "You. Me. Alone. Mmmmm." She licked her lips.

Lacy turned without looking at Sellars and led the way to the door. "Thank you, Aggie. You're the best."

Sellars gave Aggie a once-over before she followed Lacy to the car where she stood beside the driver's door, hand on hip.

"Keys, Louise." Lacy held her hand out.

Sellars stepped off the curb to join her. She held the keys just out of reach. "I'll let you drive under one condition."

"What?"

"Never make me do that again no matter how much that man is paying you. He can't change me and neither can you." She dropped the keys into Lacy's hand, aware Lacy, for once, didn't have something spiteful waiting on the tip of her tongue.

Several seconds went by, her gaze locked on Lacy's beautiful chocolate eyes, and then she walked around her and dropped into the passenger seat.

Thirty minutes later, they pulled into the Heinz Field parking lot. Sellars was impressed with the way the man at the gate waved them right in with nothing more than a nod, like this was normal for Lacy and happened often.

Lacy led the way down a few halls, a few turns, and suddenly, she was eye level with the football field. She wasn't a football fan, so she didn't share in the hype of the fanatics, but no one could miss the way the city came alive during football season, how everyone seemed to be wearing black and gold like no other colors existed. This was a prideful town, and when it came to sports, everyone seemed to become family.

Lacy kicked off her shoes on the edge of the field, pointing for Sellars to do the same.

"Before you step foot on this sacred ground, leave the bullshit drama with your shoes." Lacy cocked a daring brow at Sellars then stepped onto the grass with a sigh and walked to the fifty-yard line. She lay on her back, arms to the side, and closed her eyes.

Sellars did the same, inhaling the quiet moment. She didn't do this enough. Relax. Just breathe.

Many minutes went by before Lacy spoke. "Isn't it peaceful?"

"Only when you don't talk," Sellars mumbled.

"No other place on earth makes me feel more protected."

Sellars opened her eyes and turned to look at Lacy. She was staring up at the sky.

White, puffy clouds filled the distance, adding a touch of serenity to the moment.

"What do you need protection from?" Sellars asked, avoiding the real question. *Do your demons still haunt you, Lacy? You couldn't outrun them, could you?*

Several seconds ticked by before Lacy responded. "Do you own a Terrible Towel?"

"No." Sellars lied. She had one still in a box somewhere in the spare bedroom of her apartment. The very apartment that had been ready for her to move into for well over a month. All she needed to do was buy all new furniture, minus a bed.

She liked being at Billy's. He was like the family she'd always wished she had. The family that only existed on her television growing up. He hadn't pushed her to move out, and she was wasn't in a hurry to leave.

"How can anyone live in this city and not own a rally towel?" Lacy turned on her side to face Sellars. "You're a fucking Patriots fan, aren't you? That would explain a lot."

Sellars chuckled. "I'm not a fan of football at all."

"Figures." Lacy rolled onto her back again, her gaze straight above her. "Bet you didn't know that tough yellow towel was the first ever of its kind, created by Myron Cope, or that the proceeds from every sale go to a school for people with mental and physical disabilities, or that when he passed away, his casket was draped in a quilt made out of Terrible Towels from a fan, or that hundreds of people lined downtown in the pouring snow to wave those rally towels in his honor."

"Who is Myron Copes?" Sellars offered a sarcastic grin when Lacy snapped her head to the side to stare at her.

No one living in or near this city could avoid knowing who the sports commentator was or how he was loved by so many. His heart still beat through the town.

Lacy smirked at her mocking grin. "Before I end my vacation, I'll see that you get a proper tour of the Great Hall." Lacy looked back to the sky. "It should be a prerequisite for anyone living here."

"If you love this city so much, why is your zip code nine oh two one oh?"

"Sorry, stud." Lacy closed her eyes. "This is a drama-free zone. I'm not allowed to bring anything negative to this field."

"You called me stud." Sellars closed her own eyes to the sky. "I knew it. You like me."

"Pfft. Keep dreaming, shitface."

Chapter Seven

Sellars paced the floor in the great room. It had been three hours since a courier had delivered a large white box with *Aggie Style* in gold letters dominating the lid, and two hours since Lacy had disappeared down those stairs to get dressed for the event tonight.

What in the hell was taking her so long? She only had one head of hair, ten fingers and ten toes for nail polish, and only had one face to apply that makeup. Even Darlene, who had made it home from her business trip in time to help Lacy tonight, had been curious enough to go down into the man cave over an hour ago, and still, neither of them had emerged.

Not that she was in a hurry to attend tonight's ridiculous bigwig meeting. Her grandfather would be walking among the people, nose high, ego fat, voice loud, as always. He liked to be noticed. Liked to feel important. Liked being the loudest. The people he walked among would have deep pockets. They always did.

Her grandfather was a great businessman. Had made himself a household name in business and in NASCAR. She should be proud of him. But she couldn't be. He was dirty. He hit below the belt and cared about himself and himself alone. No one would ever taint the family name. Not even his own granddaughter. And no amount of money would stop him from cleaning up a family mess.

When the door creaked open, Sellars let out a sigh of relief, although why, she wasn't sure. The last person she wanted to spend the night with was Lacy. Her tongue was sharp as blades. But damn if she wasn't beautiful while she was cutting Sellars down to size and constantly reminding her what a fuckup she was.

All those mental smacks on the wrist had made her wet today, reminding her she needed Lacy to hurry so they could get this little shindig over with. There was a nightclub calling her name. Hopefully, the very place she would find a woman to scream it later.

Darlene stepped through the door. She smiled at Billy and Sellars. "I would do a drum roll and act out some fabulous introdu—"

Lacy pushed through the doorway, and Sellars felt the breath catch in her throat. "Like hell you will introduce me like some fucking debutante. Don't make me shift your hair extensions just a little bit."

Darlene chuckled, and Billy gave a low, admiring whistle.

Sellars stood dumbfounded. Unable to move. Unable to breathe.

She'd never seen anything more amazing. More stunning. More beautiful.

Draped in a long red chiffon dress that was cut down to her navel, Lacy was the epitome of stunning class. No. She was absolute perfection. From those spiked pumps to the diamond earrings dangling from each lobe, hair caressing her shoulders in tight curls, she was edible. Downright edible.

Darlene cleared her throat, and Sellars remembered to breathe.

"Oh dear Lord," Lacy scoffed. "Don't you dare go all man on me. It's just skin and tits, for fuck's sake. You've seen more skin in alleys." Lacy stepped around Sellars. "Now roll your tongue back in your mouth and let's get this shit night over with. Maybe I'll get lucky and find some hot butch to rip this ridiculous crap off of me later."

Sellars was held frozen in place as Lacy strode across the floor. She admired the way that dress cut all the way down to the curve of Lacy's ass. She mentally felt her hands cupping that sashaying swing, heard Lacy's sigh as she pulled her legs up and around Sellars's hips, that sharp cry as she drove inside her.

"Well, that sweet moment lasted." Billy chuckled and headed toward the kitchen.

Darlene patted Sellars on the back. "Beware. She bites. Hard. That's why we love her so much." She giggled, then turned and followed her husband.

The thirty-minute drive to the hotel was torturous. Lacy smelled so good. Flowery and sweet. Sellars was thankful that the close proximity had come to an end as she pulled up to the valet. Luckily, he escorted Lacy from the car first. Lacy would have surely hurt her feelings if she'd pulled that ridiculous stunt of trying to be a gentleman by opening her door.

And suddenly, they were both standing on the sidewalk, staring at the people walking into the lobby.

Women dressed to the nines, each of them. Diamonds twinkled under the pole lights added for extra brightness. Men stood tall in their starched white tuxedos.

The tension snaked through her gut faster than she thought possible. She didn't want to be here. Not even with a luscious date on her arm, one she knew would put each of these people in their places if they said the wrong thing.

She didn't belong here. Not among them, not with them.

"You're not gonna flake out on me, are you?" Lacy stepped in front of Sellars, forcing her gaze down into those eyes. "Sorry, that sounded like a question. It wasn't. It's an order. You will not flake out."

Sellars swallowed, forcing back the urge to lean down and kiss her. What would Lacy do? Kiss her back? Slap the shit out of her? Remind Sellars that she wasn't for sale? Oh, but she was. She wouldn't be standing on this sidewalk with her dress cut out for the world to imagine what divineness lay beneath, if Lacy didn't have a price tag.

She'd sold out to her grandfather. That was a fact.

"What good will all those walking bank accounts do me?" Sellars gave a stiff nod toward the building. "Not a single one of them even knows my name."

"Pfft. That's your wishful thinking, dumbass." Lacy tucked a curl behind her ear. "Trust me. For as many publicity stunts as you've put on for the world to see, they all know your name."

Sellars stared down over her. "Way to make me feel better."

"Oh, did you think I was here to make you feel better?" Lacy took her arm and gave an assuring squeeze then turned them toward the lobby doors. "I'm so sorry you got your wires crossed."

Sellars watched the crowd beyond the glass. Wine glasses. Champagne flutes. Stiff and proper. She hated this. Being forced to walk among them for the sake of her grandfather. For the sake of her own reputation.

Lacy followed her gaze. "Look, don't see them as people. They're cattle. Being herded by the need to feel important. To look important. But they're not, Sellars. They're just people beneath their pricy attire. People. People who can be an important role in your comeback."

Sellars glanced down at the sidewalk, catching a glimpse of Lacy's stiletto. Lacy looked that part tonight. Important. But not Sellars. She was in dark blue jeans, white T-shirt, and gray blazer. Same as she always was. She refused to change. Not for a paycheck. Not for ratings. And sure as hell not for fans who couldn't care less if she lived or died.

"Don't you dare hang your head," Lacy snapped, forcing Sellars to look up. "You did this shit to yourself. Now walk your ass in their like a fucking boss, head high, ego large, and fix it."

Sellars snickered. "You just described my grandfather."

"Oh for fuck's sake." Lacy grabbed Sellars's hand. "Let me show you a little secret before you break down and cry or some stupid shit like show a feeling."

Sellars expected to be led toward the building, hopeful that Lacy wasn't going to persuade her that stepping through those doors was in her best interest. Instead, Lacy hiked up her dress, kicked off her shoes, pulled Sellars off the curb, and together they jogged across the street.

As soon as they got safely to the other side, Lacy let go of her hand. Her palm suddenly felt cold, and she resisted grabbing those slender fingers again.

Lacy stepped onto the thick grass. "Take off your shoes and follow me." She started across the grounds.

There wasn't another living soul she wanted to follow at this moment in time. Lacy looked amazing with her tanned legs bare, the loose strands of her hair caught in the breeze, her back naked and beckoning.

Sellars kicked off her shoes and followed, pulled by the need to get to know Lacy more. To understand what made her tick. What made her so special to Billy and his family. What made Sellars want to fuck her so bad.

"I come here every vacation," Lacy said as Sellars caught up with her. "It's my miracle spot. Eases tension like nothing else."

The plush grass felt like velvet beneath her feet, and she had the urge to lie down in it, to stare up at the stars, and just be. Like she had been on the football field. Serene.

But Lacy had something else in mind as she continued to lead them toward the tunnel that opened to the grounds of the Point. A soft blue glow surrounded the bridge as they got closer.

It was a place Sellars couldn't help but notice on her nightly drives through the city, especially coming out of the Fort Pitt Tunnel. There was no other view in the world that could compare to that entrance of welcome. The fountain was always lit up in seasonal colors and brought a sense of calm to the city.

Lacy started over the bridge that crossed a large, shallow wishing pond but stopped at the top of the arch. She looked down into the water lit by several underwater light fixtures.

"This is where you can release your demons." Lacy turned a mocking smile on Sellars. "Well, you actually take pride in owning yours, obviously. But I come here to let mine go free."

Sellars stopped beside Lacy and looked down into the blue lit waters. "I was under the impression that you kind of owned your demons, too." She turned to look at Lacy, whose smile slowly faded. "Nine oh two one oh, right?"

"Scream, assface."

"Excuse me?"

"Scream, Sellars."

"What the hell for?"

Lacy turned back toward the water, grabbed hold of the bridge railing, bent forward, and screamed.

The sound echoed against the rock walls, blending in with the roar of tires crossing the freeway above them.

She took in another deep breath and repeated the scream, this time bending farther over the railing and forcing the shrill of that scream down toward the water.

When she was done, she turned toward Sellars. "Your turn."

"What good is screamin—"

"Do it!" Lacy barked.

Sellars eyed her for several seconds, looked around her to see if anyone was nearby, then behind her, where they'd come from. No one was there. Not a single living creature.

"This is silly." Sellars turned back to Lacy.

"As silly as walking around like a tightly wound ball of fury?" Lacy nodded toward the water. "Do it, chickenshit."

Sellars could only stare at her, physically fighting the need to kiss her. To hike that dress up her thighs, drop to her knees, and feast on her. She needed to taste Lacy so bad the need curled painfully in her gut.

What was it about Lacy? A woman who blatantly disliked her, who was only standing before her because someone was paying her to be here. A woman who would be gone in less than four weeks. Back to her hiding spot in the world. Who wore her demons like a prized medallion as well.

Lacy gave a firm nod. "Do it."

Sellars turned toward the water. Pennies, dimes, nickels glimmered beneath the glowing waters. Light ripples danced across the top.

She inhaled and screamed.

The sound was more like a bellow, but it felt so good she inhaled and did it again. The sound echoed around her as she took in another deep breath and roared out another scream.

Tension unwound, and she felt lighter. Less mad. Yes. She was less mad. She was always mad. At who, she never quite knew. Herself for making a poor choice so many years ago. A decision that cost a life. A life that meant the world to her. Mad for continuing to make those bad choices all these years later.

"Felt great, didn't it?" Lacy said.

Sellars turned to her. Those eyes. So rich with life. A smile teetered on her lips.

She did feel better. As hard as that was to believe. Hell, she wasn't sure the last time she felt so released. So unburdened.

Without thinking, Sellars tugged Lacy against her chest and kissed her.

Lacy felt a moment of shock as Sellars's mouth crushed against her own. Her tongue begged for entrance as her hands drove down the skin of her back, down to the curve of her ass.

Lacy parted her lips, and Sellars expelled a moan of relief. Their tongues entangled.

Lacy hummed as heat coiled tight in her gut. Her insides clamped down.

Sellars pushed in front of her, trapping Lacy against the railing. Her hands were hot against her skin as they caressed her naked back.

Lacy responded by pressing harder against her, deepening the kiss, weaving her hands into Sellars's hair.

Once again, her insides clamped down, and she groaned against those lips.

Sellars was kissing her. Her hands were exploring.

Lacy sucked in a startled breath and shoved Sellars away.

Sellars had been kissing her. She'd let her.

Her hands had been exploring. Lacy had let her.

Fuck. She'd wanted her to. And so, so much more.

What in God's name had gotten into her? She couldn't stand Sellars. Hated everything she stood for.

Yet she'd wanted that kiss. Wanted those hands wandering over her bare-naked flesh. Wanted Sellars inside her.

Lacy swiped the back of her hand across her lips as she stared at Sellars. "I'll tell you the same thing I told your grandfather. I'm not for sale."

Sellars didn't have a chance to respond as Lacy shoved around her and started back across the grass. She watched the sexy sway of her ass and smiled.

Had she really said that to her grandfather?

Did he believe her?

Did Sellars?

Everything was for sale. Everyone had a price tag. Her grandfather had taught her that hard lesson.

What had been Lacy's price?

CHAPTER EIGHT

Sellars wasn't surprised to see Lacy up, dressed, mug in hand, when she stepped through the front door. She'd spent the last hour trying to sweat the thoughts of Lacy's lips from her conscious by working on a car that never needed to be worked on. The work had been a useless attempt. She'd only managed to think more, taking that kiss far beyond where it ended in her alone time. She was always more dangerous when alone, with her thoughts, with her memories and all the pain they dragged to the surface. It wasn't surprising that the fantasy of Lacy could bring on just as much pain, just in a different body region.

They'd driven home last night in complete silence. For some sick reason, it gave her pleasure to know that she'd rendered Lacy speechless. She was positive not too many people had achieved that goal.

But today was a new day, and if Lacy wanted to pretend that kiss never happened, then she would have to play along. There was no need to twist things any tighter than they needed to be.

Not to mention, they had a busy day ahead of them at the local soup kitchen feeding the homeless. It wasn't her idea of a great day, but she had a feeling Lacy would be pleased. Had a feeling this was Lacy's doing, not her grandfather's.

Without making eye contact, Sellars headed directly for the stairs. "Be back in fifteen."

Lacy didn't respond. She kept her sight trained on the pool beyond the sliding doors as Sellars disappeared up to the second floor.

She didn't really know how to respond. She'd kissed Sellars. She'd liked it. Thought about doing it again all night. Worse, the house had been empty except for the two of them. Billy, Darlene, and Gabby had left last night, earlier than planned, for their mini vacation with Grandma. She would be alone with Sellars for the rest of the week, maybe longer, and that made her nervous as hell.

Not because she didn't want to be alone with her, but because she didn't trust herself to be alone with her. She'd already made a mistake by not slapping the shit out of her. For responding to that kiss. For wanting more. For fucking needing more than just that kiss.

She was still sipping coffee and staring blankly through the window when Sellars cleared her throat from beside her chair.

"You ready to get this over with?"

Lacy turned a skeptical eye on her, not missing that her hair had been towel dried, that she was wearing stonewashed jeans that matched her blazer. Or that the cream colored T-shirt was slick against her body, leaving little to Lacy's imagination.

Lord help her. It was going to be a long day outrunning her dirty thoughts.

"You got something against feeding people who would gladly kiss your Converse tennis shoes for a fucking tiny bite of food? Who are lucky just to have a goddamn pair of grungy shoes on their feet, let alone own something with a name brand attached to it?"

"Whoa. Whoa." Sellars held her hands up defensively. "I wasn't referring to the homeless."

Lacy took the last sip of coffee, set it down with a bang, then stood to face her. "What exactly were you referring to?"

Sellars swallowed.

Lacy looked so daring. So sexy in her tight jeans and v-neck T-shirt that made Sellars struggle not to look down into her cleavage. Normally, she'd have done just that. Women seemed to like when she admired them, openly, even if it was a jackass move that was nothing more than belittling. But it never stopped her from showing the disrespect. Nor did it ever stop them from letting Sellars take them home.

But somehow, she knew Lacy would only add it to her ever growing pile of dimwit things she'd done.

"You, having to suffer through your day, shadowing me."

"How sweet." Lacy slapped several bills on the counter next to the swear jar. "Then by all means, let's get this over with."

Lacy moved around her just to put the distance between them. Sellars smelled so damn good. Delicious. She smelled delicious. And it was definitely time to visit some local night-clubs. Her insides couldn't take much more of this clamping.

In the driveway, Sellars stalled at the car and pulled the keys from her pocket. "Should I offer to drive? I know how much that ruffles your feathers."

Lacy walked to her, plucked the keys from her grasp, and continued to the driver's door. "Offer away. But I'm driving." She dropped into the seat, inserted the key, and cranked the car.

Sellars got in and closed the door as Lacy revved the engine. She wanted to add some comments. First, to tell Lacy to chill out with the gas pedal. Second, to tell her how sexy she looked behind the wheel.

Neither comment would end without a tongue lashing so she kept them to herself and enjoyed the drive to the city. She never actually got to view it from the passenger window. The buildings loomed in the distance. Sexy. Even the city was sexy. Not to mention, everyone was gearing up for the playoffs. Flags bearing the Steelers logo were already adorning poles in various businesses as well as residents' yards. Soon, the hype would be all around them. Every Sunday, the city was filled with crowds looking to watch the game from their favorite restaurants, or joining the line of traffic backed up to get across the bridge for the field.

What did Lacy do on Sundays from across the map where the weather never required hoodies? Did she hang with friends at some local sports club? Maybe watch the game from her TV with a significant other? Did she even have someone special in her life? It was a question she hadn't thought about until now. Billy had never mentioned anyone other than Lacy. Never Lacy along with someone else.

"What do you do for fun in LA?" Sellars asked before she could stop herself.

"Depends on your definition of fun." Lacy moved down the off-ramp and merged into the city traffic.

"I need to decipher the definition of fun?" Sellars snickered. "Well, that answers my next question."

"Which is?" Lacy stopped at the red light and turned her gaze on Sellars.

Another mistake. Looking at Sellars. She was downright casual and sexy as fucking sin.

"If there was a girlfriend in the picture."

"And because my idea of fun and your idea of fun may be two different ideas, you assume I don't have a girlfriend?" Lacy turned to look at the light only because those eyes were luring her into dirty thoughts again. If they had ever stopped.

She needed sex like a drug addict needed her next fix. She was almost desperate for relief. Tonight, she would go after that itch scratcher. There was no other choice if she was going to survive the next few days of hanging with Sellars.

"You have taken away all assumptions. I know you don't," Sellars said.

Lacy chuckled. "True. I don't have a girlfriend. By choice." She pushed the clutch in and shifted the gear into drive as the light changed to green. "Not that it's any of your business."

"It's not."

"Exactly." Lacy continued to the next red light.

"Exactly."

"Were you worried that some jealous girlfriend was going to come stomp your ass?" Lacy tapped her finger on the steering wheel, clearly agitated.

"I never worry about anything."

"Clearly."

"Clearly."

"Shouldn't you? Worry?"

"Worry about what?" Sellars looked into the sky at the building tops, trying to appear nonchalant.

"A fucking mean ass girlfriend."

"You shouldn't stay with a mean ass girlfriend."

"I don't have a mean…" Lacy huffed. "I don't have a girlfriend. At all!"

"Clearly."

"Oh my God. Just shut the hell up, Sellars."

"No problem."

"Seriously. Just zip it."

"Zipped."

Lacy was fuming by the time they pulled into the soup kitchen parking lot. So much for always needing to have the last word. She was so mad she couldn't even think of words. Actually, there were no words. Just actions. Actions like climbing into Sellars's lap and grinding until an orgasm ripped through her body. Actions like dropping her chair back, hiking her legs around her face, and pumping against her mouth.

That mouth. Oh, she wanted that mouth clamped around her clit nursing and sucking, making her arch and bow and scream.

The light turned green.

Flustered with her heated thoughts, Lacy popped the clutch and the car died.

"Fuck!" She quickly cranked the car and steadily pulled forward as to not embarrass herself for a second time.

Sex. She needed sex. Fast and in a fucking hurry.

Finally, they arrived at the soup kitchen. Neither of them spoke as they stepped inside the building.

"Lacy!" Annabelle yelled as she made her way around the buffet counter. "It's so great to see your pretty face."

Sellars watched them hug, wondering if this was yet another woman Lacy had fucked on one of her yearly vacations to Pittsburgh.

A jealous seed planted itself in her gut as the hug continued.

Lacy finally pulled away and turned to Sellars. "This is our delinquent."

Annabelle gave Lacy a scoff and stuck her hand out to Sellars. She gripped the woman's hand just a little tighter than necessary.

Lacy was starting to push her nerves. Every one of them. Especially the ones that connected her common sense to her sexual desire. Yes. That one. That one Lacy was tromping on. Right now, with Lacy watching her with that mischievous look in her eye, she wasn't sure any other nerves existed anymore.

"Sellars, thank you so much for joining us today. It means a lot." Annabelle smiled.

If she'd fucked Lacy, it didn't show in her expression like it had with Aggie.

"As much as I would love the credit for being honorable, this wasn't my decision. It's my punishment." Sellars finally dragged her sights away from Lacy.

"Trust me, these people don't care." Annabelle clapped Sellars on the back and walked them toward the kitchen. "You could be a serial killer and they'd be grateful. We're all heroes to them."

Sellars considered her words as Annabelle explained how the assembly line would work, to mingle among everyone, check glasses, ask if they needed anything else, to smile and relax because they were all harmless, and if she found herself locked in a conversation, to consider herself lucky because most of them didn't offer much about their life.

"Well, except for Miss Lacy here. They seem to think she is one of their own. They tell her their whole life story." Annabelle said with a smile.

Lacy shrugged. "What can I say? They think I'm their therapist."

An hour later, Lacy was standing near the back of the room, camera trained on Sellars as she refilled drinks at one of the tables. The lens couldn't hide the fact that Sellars was out of her element. Her expression showed it. This wasn't her cup of tea. Probably due to her upbringing. The silver spoon baby who was no doubt taught that the homeless were dangerous, to stand back, walk around them, don't make eye contact.

Hopefully, the photos wouldn't display her comfort level. Her fans, or the ones that could possibly be lured back, a process she'd already started with the first round of photos she had posted, would see right through the staged bullshit. Mr. Reynolds might have meant well when he arranged this little photo op, but if he thought spooning food onto a plate for a line of homeless people was going to win back some hearts, he was sadly mistaken.

It would take more than a little fake compassion to undo the damage Sellars had done to herself.

At least she was being a good sport. Lacy had captured a few smiles, a few deep conversations, about what, she wasn't sure, and she captured Sellars actually sitting down beside someone.

That action said a lot about her character. Most of the volunteers never sat with them. Never struck up a conversation. Not like Lacy had. Not like Sellars had.

If she had to confess to herself, she was proud of Sellars for going through with the day.

"Lacy, I have all the food packed up and ready for you." Annabelle sidled up next to Lacy. "And your girl, she did good. She even got ole Henry to talk."

Lacy continued to snap the pictures as Sellars laughed at something someone said. "She probably promised him a seat at a race that she won't be at come the new season."

"I've seen worse people come back from the grave."

Lacy didn't comment. Sellars was a dead man walking and everyone knew it. Even if Lacy found a way to keep her out of trouble for the next three weeks, there were many more after that. She'd surely fall right back into her old habits once the green flag was back in motion. It was her motto.

But in the meantime, Lacy was going to keep going like her future wasn't riding on the hopes that Sellars could pull off the impossible. Her project depended on it. Homeless men and women depended on it. Somehow, she had to make it to the finish line so Sellars could make it to the start line. After that, she could crash and burn for all Lacy cared.

"Speaking of grave, have you seen Ralph?"

"Actually, I haven't. But you know how he is about crowds." Annabelle patted her arm and scurried away to check on another table.

Sellars worked her way toward Lacy. She wasn't uncomfortable, per se, but she definitely couldn't wait to call this a day. It was rather sad to see how many people were truly only looking for a meal. No one had asked her for money or a hand out. They just wanted someone to see them. To talk to them. To hear what they had to say.

That was sad. They had nothing. No one. This building, with food from donations and volunteers, could be the only comfort in their world.

"Have you snapped enough pictures?" Sellars asked as Lacy lowered the camera.

"Are you being a smartass?"

"According to you, that's my normal behavior. Wouldn't want to let you down," Sellars added a wink.

Lacy shifted to ease the sudden burn. Sex. That nightclub. Very soon. It was a must.

"I have one more job for you." Lacy took a step forward and pursed her lips.

Sellars took a step forward as well, erasing the single foot between, angling her sights down over Lacy. "Will my hands get dirty?"

Lacy smiled and let her gaze slip to Sellars's lips. She'd kissed those lips. She couldn't stand the person attached to them. "No. But those knees, however, can't say the same for them."

She angled the camera up between them and snapped the picture. She had no idea what kind of image she had just frozen in time, but she needed sound, something, anything, to erase that look of lust and need from Sellars's face.

The sound did nothing to erase that penetrating stare.

Sellars leaned down, her lips only inches from Lacy's. "It's where I do my best work. When someone can get me there, that is."

Finally, Sellars moved back, her expression serious and calculated.

Maybe Lacy had gone too far. Flirting. She hadn't meant to. Or had she? She wasn't sure anymore. But what she was sure of, the people in this room depended on her to keep Sellars out of trouble, and if it took a little teasing to achieve that goal, then she would. Again and again and again.

To end the spell, she wrapped the strap of the camera around her neck. "Good. I was hoping you would say that. Let's go."

Sellars's insides tightened as Lacy moved around her. If only they weren't in public, she would have taken that little teasing monster and proven that she wasn't one to be toyed with. Lacy would be the one sinking to her knees. She had the exact spot for that poisonous tongue.

She watched Lacy walk away, feeling like a puppet on strings, eager to see what the next mission held for her. Besides, she wanted to get outside in the sunshine, away from these lonely faces with their sad stories of life, hardships, and loss. She wanted to walk on the sidewalk and remind herself that she was fortunate.

But fortunate how? In her life? Sarah didn't have a life. Sellars had made sure of that.

"Get out of your own head and grab these bags," Lacy said, pulling Sellars out of her thoughts only to realize she was still standing in the same spot where Lacy had left her.

She straightened, cleared her throat, cleared her mind, grabbed boxes from Annabelle, and followed Lacy out into the sunshine.

Instead of going to the car, Lacy started down the sidewalk, bags dangling from her fingertips.

"You gonna share where we're headed?" Sellars asked. "Or tell me what's in these boxes and bags?"

"To the alley. And food."

"What in the world for?"

Lacy continued her hurried steps. "Because you like alleys." She stopped at the entrance between two buildings and nodded down the alley. "And they need food."

Sellars followed her gaze. Dumpsters and trash and stacks of pallets littered the aisle. But at the very end, where she assumed linked to another street, she could make out cardboard boxes propped against the brick.

Without waiting, Lacy started down the alley, dodging broken bottles and paper cups, rotten food and dead rats.

Sellars hesitantly followed, curling her nose at the aroma of urine and rot.

Lacy didn't seem bothered by it. She kept walking like she had designed the layout herself.

When Sellars followed her around the corner, she almost gasped in surprise as the area opened up into a back alley parking lot filled with makeshift tents made from worn tarps, blankets, some even erected out of tattered clothing and rope.

Several barrels blazing with fire decorated the center, and she was shocked at how clear the asphalt was compared to the wreckage they had just walked through.

At least twelve, maybe thirteen people stood around the fire, talking and laughing with each other as if they were hanging out in some local bar, catching up on life.

"Phillip!" Lacy squealed.

A man turned from the group, and his dirty cheeks lifted in a smile to expose yellow teeth. He wore a pair of sandals that once held a logo long erased by excessive wear and tear.

Phillip jogged toward Lacy and wrapped her in a bear hug. "I knew it wouldn't be long before we saw your pretty face. How have you been, sweetheart?" He let her go and glanced at Sellars. "Who's your special friend? I say special with the utmost respect since you've never brought a living soul down into our domain."

Lacy turned to look at Sellars and considered her response. "Up. I brought her *up* into your domain. She needed to see some light."

Light was exactly what she saw.

The way Lacy sat down on aged and broken chairs to eat with them like a holiday gathering.

For an hour, she listened to their conversation about each other, how Candy's sister had found her and taken her home, how they were all so excited for her. How Carlisle had eaten something bad and had to be rushed to the hospital for food poisoning. How a group of punk boys had beat up one of the newbies, left him for dead, and he'd gone back to live with his parents.

The stories continued. All in innocent conversation. Each story shedding more light on the hell they had to endure just to survive, with Lacy snapping occasional pictures.

By the time Lacy led Sellars back to the Point, this time to the fountain, where the three rivers merged to create the Ohio, her heart was heavy with knowledge.

These people were pitiful. They needed help. More help than Lacy could give by opening a McDonald's account for them when or if they needed a little something more than the free meal at the soup kitchen could provide. More than the soup kitchen could offer on a daily basis.

She wasn't sure what more could be done, but it left a mark on her thoughts as Lacy sat on the edge of the fountain and dangled her feet in the water.

Sellars sat beside her, taking in the smooth autumn colors of the water. Just last month, the fountain had been dyed pink. Next month, it would alternate between green, red, and blue for Christmas. Another thing she loved about the city. How festive they were.

"Thank you for being cool today," Lacy said as she stared across the river at Heinz Field.

"Am I not always cool?" Sellars said. She wasn't sure how to respond. Did Lacy not think she was cool? Had she not already proven otherwise?

Of course she had. She'd proven that and more thanks to her need to self-destruct.

"How many rivers are here?" Lacy asked.

"Umm. Is this a trick question?"

"No. I'm just curious if you know the answer."

"Three? Isn't that why the old stadium was named Three Rivers?"

Lacy splashed a lazy stream of water with her red-tipped toes. "So you do pay attention." She smiled and circled those toes in the water. "But there are actually four rivers. An underground aquifer, nicknamed the fourth river, built naturally by glaciers and sheets of ice that left sand and gravel behind to choke off the riverbed. You are looking at it." She nodded toward the fountain.

Sellars looked up at the water shooting high in the sky. "Never heard that one before. I think you may be full of crap."

"When you're not too busy getting yourself into trouble, look it up. Google doesn't lie." Lacy turned serious eyes on her. "Just do it after I leave. I have a promise to keep."

"What promise is that?" Sellars admired those gorgeous eyes, the fact that Lacy loved this city so much, and that beneath that spiteful mouth, she adored her family.

Lacy shrugged and glanced back to the water.

Sellars had so many things she wanted to ask Lacy, but only one came to the surface.

"Why did you run, Lacy?" Sellars blurted the question before she could change her mind.

She watched Lacy's lips tighten and knew she'd crossed a line. Expected Lacy to scream that it was none of her fucking business. Exact words.

Lacy had made it clear that she had no desire to talk about her demons.

Without a word, Lacy slowly stood and grabbed her shoes from the edge. "Time to go. We have a busy day tomorrow."

Sellars wanted to pull her back, to say she was sorry, to tell her she didn't need the answer or to even talk at all. Instead, she followed Lacy, silently cursing her need to get to know a little more of her.

The drive back to Billy's was spent in silence when all Sellars truly wanted to do was pull over, pull Lacy into her lap, and fuck her.

The need was getting so strong it was making her ache in places she didn't think could ache anymore.

Oh, how bad they ached.

CHAPTER NINE

L acy followed Sellars under the canopy at the high school football field where the fundraiser had been set up. She set her bag down and snapped several pictures as Sellars quietly began unpacking boxes and hanging T-shirts and hoodies on the display rack.

The day would be a long one, she knew. Sellars had been moody all morning indicating she was in her head once again.

What was in there? What dark secrets made her drift inside herself so often? Were the dirty deeds that rested in the darkness the reason she acted out so often? Had they made her this reckless misfit?

Lacy hated to admit that she actually missed the sarcastic banter between them. No witty humor. No money in the swear jar. She didn't even stall when Lacy plucked the keys from her grasp in the driveway. Not a single grunt.

Or maybe it had more to do with being here, at this NASCAR function, among the other racers, people who disliked her for good reasons. Not one person had said hello to her or even helped her locate the gear she would be selling. Was it eating at her? That she'd created this rift between them by being such a careless asshole?

Fans were already beginning to mingle, yet her tent remained unoccupied. No one had asked for an autograph or checked out the memorabilia.

Did she regret that she had only herself to blame for their dislike? For their blatant hatred?

For the first time since they'd met, Lacy felt a pang of pity for her. She was in this game all alone. Of course she'd put herself there. But right now, that was beside the point, and Lacy didn't plan to spend her entire day in stuffy silence.

"Why don't you go out and mingle with the people? Maybe greet some fans," Lacy said.

"Why don't you put that camera down and help hang this crap up?" Sellars barked.

Lacy snapped a picture, then another, and another, until Sellars gave her a scowl. "Because I'm not the star of this show." She shielded the sun from her eyes and looked around dramatically. "But then again, looks like you aren't the star either."

"Screw you." Sellars yanked a hoodie onto a hanger then jammed it on the rack.

"Ooh. Do we have touchy feelings today?" Lacy let the camera hang from the strap around her neck. "Is da baby upset that no one wikes her?"

"Suits me fine. I don't like people, anyway." Sellars slammed another hanger onto the rack.

"Liar, liar, pants on fire." Lacy grabbed a hanger and started helping. "It bothers you a lot."

"No, it doesn't." Sellars glared at her.

Truth was, she really didn't care. Maybe she should, but she didn't. Wasn't that the problem? She never had. Well, maybe once she might have. But not anymore. Their opinions, the fans, her opposing racers, didn't matter at all to her. Only her own opinion meant anything and she couldn't think any less of herself, so why should their hatred intervene?

Sellars's gaze landed over her shoulder, and a mask of anger drifted across her expression.

Lacy slowly turned to find three racers standing behind her, all wearing their own sponsor T-shirts. She recognized one of them immediately. The racer whose wife had been photographed in the alley with Sellars.

Brett Inman. New king of the track, though there was only one true king of any track in Lacy's eyes. Richard Petty, long retired from the racing world, would forever hold that title. Like Richard, Brett was an amazing racer who seemed to be collecting trophies. Unlike Richard, he was a brazen asshole who didn't deserve a single one.

And his appearance obviously wasn't going to end well.

"Shit," Lacy mumbled.

"Come on, man. Let's keep it moving," one of the other men said.

"Kip Sellars," Brett growled. "Didn't think you'd show your sorry face here today."

Sellars cocked that sarcastic smile. "I think I have a rather handsome face." She propped her hand up on the end of the rack and appeared cool. "Pretty sure you'll find a few others who agree. Just ask around."

Brett took a step forward, and the two other men stuck their arms out. "You're not wanted here, you outcast!" His teeth ground tightly together as he pushed against the men's arms. "You need to go the fuck away while you can still walk away on your own two feet!"

Sellars chuckled while Lacy's heart raced. "Threatening to take my feet out from under me, Brett? I can see why you'd be threatened by them. Seeing how they're made of lead." She shrugged, her expression unreadable. "But don't be afraid of losing, my man." Her jaw tightened. "Because I'm coming for you."

Lacy took a step toward Sellars, unsure why she did it, somehow knowing she needed to. As much as Sellars played by her own rules, something deep down inside told her she might have a fighting chance of stopping Sellars when this got ugly. And it would get ugly. She was positive of it.

"Bring it, faggot!" Brett pushed against the men again, gaining a few inches toward Sellars.

Sellars cut her sights on Lacy and she laughed. "Look at this guy showing his education and maturity." She turned back to Brett and the laugh vanished. "How's that tasty wife of yours?"

Ah, shit.

"You fucking bitch!" Brett shoved and pushed against the men, arms flailing. "I'm going to rip your faggot head off!"

Sellars never moved from her relaxed position as he withered, attempting to push through the strong arms holding him back.

"Don't be such a spoilsport, man. I left plenty of meat for you."

Brett relaxed, his glare more daring than it was angry. He moved back and shucked off one of the men. "That's more than I can say about your girlfriend." He lifted his chin like he was proud of his comeback.

Lacy glanced up at Sellars. Her jaw was clenched again. Fire sparked in her expression.

"How much fun did you have scooping up her body pieces from the asphalt, you fucking cunt!" Spittle flew from his mouth.

Sellars pushed off the rack before Lacy knew she was in flight.

"Sellars! No!" Lacy screamed.

The sound of her plea was swallowed in Sellars's agonized roar. She charged at him, breaking past the first man who tried to intervene by blocking her path.

She didn't stall as she reared her fist back, pushed the other man aside with her free hand, and punched Brett square in the face. And again. And again.

The men bellowed as they dove for Sellars.

The sound drew attention from other people. They raced toward the fight, cell phones angled, and seconds seemed to tick by while they struggled to drag Sellars off Brett.

She was still swinging when they pulled her backward, her face contorted with rage. Her teeth ground tight, her eyes narrowed and trained on Brett.

"I'm coming for you, mother fucker!" Sellars screamed.

It was the first time Lacy had even heard her cuss and mentally reminded herself to make sure Sellars paid that swear jar accordingly.

Brett wiped blood from his nose and mouth. "You'll find me in your windshield, bitch!"

Lacy finally found her footing and her thoughts. Trouble. This was bad. She was supposed to be keeping Sellars out of trouble, not watching her get into it.

She grabbed Sellars's arm and tugged her backward. "Sellars. Stop it! Please!"

Sellars's glare was still pasted forward, daring him, anyone, to make a move.

Lacy had never seen anyone so angry in her life.

She stepped in front of Sellars and put her hands against her chest. "Sellars!"

For several seconds, Sellars stared over her head, eyes trained on him, and finally, she looked down at Lacy.

"Stop it." Lacy smoothed her hand down Sellars's arms. "Take his ass out on the track, okay? This isn't the place."

Sellars watched her for several seconds, and with a final glance in his direction, she barged out from under the canopy.

Lacy turned toward the men and let her gaze walk over each of their faces before she stalled on Brett. "I hope your calculated and premeditated visit ended exactly how you wanted." She gave an admiring whistle when Brett wiped more blood from his lips. "You'll need ice for that swelling, dumbass."

She didn't give any of them a chance to speak before she charged after Sellars

She finally caught up with her at the car, already behind the wheel, hands gripped tight on the steering wheel.

Lacy hesitantly dropped into the passenger seat and waited, unsure what to say, knowing full well it was only a matter of time before she asked about the girlfriend. No way she could let a statement, or a reaction, go without being nosy.

Minutes passed while Sellars continued to loosen and tighten her grip. Lacy wanted to say something, anything, but she was more worried that the sound of her voice would do more harm than good.

"Buckle!" Sellars barked.

Lacy only stared, confused by the single word, until Sellars turned those sexy green eyes on her.

"Buckle!" Sellars barked again.

Lacy finally understood the word for what it meant. A command. To buckle up.

As soon as the metal clicked together, Sellars slammed the clutch down, shoved the stick into drive, and pulled away from the parking space.

Lacy expected tires to squeal. Expected to be thrown around the car like a rag doll. Instead, Sellars obeyed every speed limit as she made her way out of the city and onto the back roads, seeming to be going nowhere in particular.

"Two roads up, take a right," Lacy finally said after too much time of silence.

To her surprise, Sellars slowed down and turned onto the dead end street.

"When you come to the split in the road, veer right," Lacy said.

This was a place she came to almost every vacation. It was a quiet spot down a long dirt road, set back in the woods overlooking a wide creek.

It was the perfect place to capture all of Sellars's anger. The very images she'd envisioned capturing from the second she laid eyes on her.

When the dirt path ended, Sellars stopped the car and killed the engine. "If you wanted me alone, all you had to do was say so."

Lacy opened her door. "Get out, asshole."

Sellars got out, slammed the door, and met Lacy at the front of the car with a scowl on her face.

Lacy snapped the first picture.

"Will you get that damn thing out of my face?" Sellars growled.

"Show me, Sellars." Lacy took a few steps back, lens trained on that enraged expression. "Show me that anger."

Sellars stopped her slow pace to stare at Lacy. "What the hell are you doing?"

Lacy continued to snap. "Capturing the real you. The mad, hate the whole fucking world, you. That's the person you want us all to see, right?" She moved backward again but zoomed the lens in.

Sellars was so damn sexy. Her hair hung in her face, masking those green eyes into lustful pits of darkness.

"I don't hate the whole world." Sellars kicked a pine cone across the path.

"Who do you hate, Sellars?" Lacy stepped closer. "Your granddaddy? Mommy? Daddy?" She took another step and snapped. "Take off your jacket."

Sellars arched a brow at her. "Now you're talking my language." She shucked out of the blazer and tossed it on the roof.

"Take that fucking shirt off, too."

The lens hummed.

"My pleasure, sexy." Sellars peeled the T-shirt over her head.

Lacy licked her lips behind the camera as the delicious view of Sellars's body bloomed in front of her. A mean set of abs greeted her zoom; buff, strong arms; and dear God, there were detailed cut marks disappearing down into those jeans. Not to mention the starched white sports bra that was bright against her tanned skin.

Sex. She was sexually deprived and needed to alleviate that particular situation in the near future. The nightclub was screaming her name as she kept depressing the shutter.

"Sit on the edge of the hood," Lacy commanded.

Sellars did as told, and Lacy stepped closer.

"The racers can't stand you," Lacy said.

"I don't care."

"The fans hate you."

"I don't care."

"Say something to them, Sellars. Show them all what you think about them."

Sellars shot her a bird, her expression set.

Lacy snapped several more shots, easing closer, or being pushed. She wasn't sure anymore. Only that she needed to capture this moment.

"Yes. That's it." Lacy snapped another picture. "Fuck you, world! Fuck you, fans. Fuck you, Granddaddy."

Sellars raised her other hand and gave the same salute with the other finger. Her lips curled back in another snarl.

"Oh yeah." Lacy squatted down near the bumper to get another angle. "I'm Kip Sellars, and I don't give a good goddamn about your opinions."

Sellars lowered her arms but continued to stare at the camera.

Lacy rose. "Tell me about the girlfriend, Sellars."

Lacy regretted the request, the dying desire to meet Sellars's demon, as soon as her lips thinned into a grim line in the viewfinder, and then she pushed off the hood.

CHAPTER TEN

Sellars dropped off the car, her heart racing, her gut knotted, and tugged the camera from Lacy's grasp.

Lacy turned her chin up in defiance. Defiance that only fueled Sellars's rage.

How dare this woman poke into her secrets? Into her heart.

Sellars trained the camera on Lacy's face and circled around her. "Let's talk about your skeletons, Lacy." She started walking forward, forcing Lacy to walk backward.

"I don't have any skeletons. My life is practically an open book. Especially with Billy blurting everything." Lacy smirked.

"Is that so?" Sellars continued walking forward. "Is this the camera you used? The one you used to freeze-frame death?"

Lacy's smirk vanished and her expression changed to anger. "Fuck you."

"Ah. Yes. There it is." Sellars pressed the button on the camera. "The ghost in the machine. The demon you can never outrun. Isn't that right, Lacy?"

Lacy reached for the camera, but Sellars ducked backward. "Give me the fucking camera."

"Why? You were so eager to capture my demon, weren't you? So eager for me to air my dirty laundry." Sellars snapped another picture. "Let's talk about your skeleton instead."

She continued walking Lacy backward when all she truly wanted to do was drop. Right there. To her knees. She wanted to open Lacy up. Wanted to feast on her. Drink from her. Taste her.

"How much blood money did you earn, Lacy?" Sellars snapped more pictures, seeing through the lens that Lacy was enraged. "Couple hundred thousand? More?" The shutter hummed. "No. Not Lacy. She likes that big money. The cha-ching! You went straight to the top, didn't you? Only millions would do for the proof hidden inside this contraption."

"Fuck you, Sellars," Lacy growled. "You don't know what the fuck you're talking about. Now give me the goddamn camera!"

Sellars continued walking toward her, pressing the button, capturing that beautiful rage. "I heard the rumors. All of them. How you sold the pictures to his family. How you leaked them to the press before the money could even get cozy in your bank account. Yep. I heard them all. And we all know how reliable those rumors are. Isn't that right, sweetheart?"

Lacy's legs buckled against the bumper and Sellars stopped walking. She trained the camera on Lacy's lips and snapped another picture.

"Go to hell," Lacy whispered.

Sellars moved the camera from her face.

Lacy looked so vulnerable trapped against the car, her eyes moist, her lips set in a narrow line. For the first time, Sellars saw the pain in those eyes. The pain Lacy forced herself to ignore. Or maybe she had convinced herself that it was part of life now. That the pain was part of life. Just like Sellars had accepted that her own pain was a permanent part of her life.

Sellars wanted to part those lips with her tongue. Wanted to hear a cry of release roll over them.

She slid the strap through her fingers and let the camera slowly drop to the ground beside her.

Lacy chewed her bottom lip, and her angered breaths grew shallow as she locked her sights on Sellars. Lust danced in her eyes.

"I can't go to hell, Lacy." Sellars pressed herself between Lacy's thighs. There was no stopping herself now. Her thoughts had already gone too far. She had no choice but to make them reality. "I'm already here. I've been here for many years. Long, endless days of hell."

"Then drop dead!" Lacy pushed her hands against Sellars's chest.

Sellars grabbed her wrists and leaned forward, not thinking, just bittersweet need coiling tight. There was no thinking left to do. No words left to say. No anger or rebellion left to give.

Lacy hummed all the way to her soul as Sellars crushed their lips together, her wrists still clamped tight in that powerful grip. She instinctively ground against her, desperate to feel Sellars's weight pinning her down, driving deep inside. More afraid that she would react to that inner voice screaming out a warning, demanding that she stop Sellars.

As if Sellars could feel her indecision, she pushed against Lacy, climbing up the bumper until Lacy was flat against the hood with Sellars hovering above her. She pinned her arms above her head and deepened the kiss.

That warning voice bellowed in her mind. Begging her to end this. To not let Sellars make another move.

She wanted to listen. She wanted to obey. Needed to obey. That voice was right. Sellars was nothing to her. Meant nothing. Amounted to nothing. She would always be the reckless destroyer of her own future. And she was going to do it with that sexy smile on her face.

Yet Lacy couldn't obey. She was without willpower to reject the promises that lay beneath those grinding hips. The selfish, idiotic part of her would win every time.

Sellars pulled back and stared down over her, her breaths hard, her eyes pleading.

"Do it," Lacy said.

A mocking smile creased Sellars's mouth.

Fuck.

She tugged her wrists free and fisted her fingers into Sellars's hair then pulled her back down, giving in to the guttural desire. That desperate, pulsing ache.

Sellars drove against her and Lacy cried out.

She needed Sellars. Needed her fingers buried deep. Needed release so bad it made her throb to the very core.

Lacy withered, desperate for Sellars's to finish her, for Sellars to pull incoherent babbling from her mouth.

Sellars pulled back and Lacy immediately missed the passion of those lips. She ripped open the rivet on Lacy's jeans and tugged the zipper down.

"Yes. Hurry! Before I come to my senses."

"You won't." Without stalling, she lifted Lacy's hips off the hood and jerked the denim down her legs.

She slowed her hurried need long enough for Lacy to kick off her ankle boots before ripping the denim down over her feet. She tossed the jeans to the ground and looked back to Lacy for confirmation.

Lacy wanted to scream hell yes. And please.

In those eyes, she saw something else. Pure lust. Her lips parted. Her chest heaving. Lacy wasn't sure the last time she'd seen passion so thick, so vibrant and at surface level.

But there it was resting on the face of someone who detested her. Someone who was only here because she had no other choice if she wanted her career back. Someone who would be gone, out of her life, very soon.

"Don't you dare fucking stop now!" Lacy barked.

Sellars dropped off the car, pulled Lacy to the edge of the hood, shoved her legs apart, and clamped her mouth around Lacy's clit.

Lacy cried out as Sellars nursed. Her hips surged upward as Sellars sucked harder, flicking her tongue, jerking Lacy toward that sexual abyss.

She clutched at Sellars's hair, her insides tight, that little voice all but silent now as the tingling sensations overcame her.

Sellars pinned her legs apart and hummed, grinding her mouth against her pussy.

Lacy came in a blinding fury of spasms. She arched against the hood as Sellars continued to suck and flick, wrapping her strong arms around Lacy's legs, holding her in place, until Lacy fell back with a dramatic sigh, her insides still twitching, her body depleted.

Finally, Sellars loosened her hold and stood between Lacy's parted thighs, her palms wide as they caressed Lacy's hips. "If I had known fucking you would make you silent, I would have done it in the jailhouse parking lot."

Lacy opened her eyes and rose on her elbows. "You call that fucking?"

That smile creased Sellars's lips again, and Lacy resisted a squirm. "Not at all." She teased her opening with the tips of two fingers, and Lacy held her breath for entry. "I call this fucking." She drove inside.

Sellars's insides clenched as Lacy threw her head back with a hiss. She pulled out to the knuckles and drove inside again, eager to keep Lacy in this state of mind where her tongue wasn't sharp and her eyes didn't despise her.

She hated that the most. Lacy's hatred floating on the surface at all times. Lacy didn't know her. Didn't know her secrets. Didn't know her past. Didn't know what she was made of or what she had accomplished. What she had yet to accomplish.

Yet right now, with those cries of passion, her lips silenced and those eyes closed, Sellars felt at peace. No memories to haunt her. No burdens weighing on her shoulders.

Nothing. Not a single thing mattered.

Lacy met every stroke, her hips driving down, swallowing Sellars.

Sellars fucked her harder, driving into her, against her, until Lacy tugged her down.

She locked her legs and arms around Sellars, her pussy clenching her fingers, and then she arched and screamed out again, bucking beneath Sellars's weight.

Sellars held her until she went limp in her grasp, an overwhelming sense of peace surrounding her. Birds chirped in the distance. The stream trickled beyond the trees. The wind was a gentle breeze.

Yet a tornado was beneath her, coming around her fingers, and it made her ache for the peace she would never have again.

"Don't say a fucking word, Sellars." Lacy attempted to bark, but the sound came out as a mumbled, no punch command.

There were no words she could say. Not out loud, anyway.

She admired Lacy's beautiful face, her gaze to the sky, indecision in her expression, and she wondered how many people had ever said those words to her. How many of those had only said it in the throes of passion. How many had wanted to say it forever.

Did Lacy want someone to say it forever? Had she ever met someone she wanted to spend eternity with?

Sellars had. Inside, she craved that calm life that someone had once promised to her. The life Sarah promised to her.

And there she was again. Sarah. Squeezing through her thoughts. As always.

Lacy turned those pretty eyes her way and Sellars suddenly felt insecure. Lacy knew her secret. Knew about Sarah. Maybe she didn't know the facts, the how, the why, or the when, but she knew enough.

Sellars didn't know what to say, if anything. Didn't know what to do, if anything.

And then she saw it. The mistake written in Lacy's eyes. In her silence. They had crossed a line that couldn't be uncrossed. Deep down, she knew these few moments with Lacy, were the only ones she might get.

She slid off the hood so she wouldn't have to see that puzzled expression another second.

Lacy sat up, grabbed Sellars's wrist, and pulled her close. She slid her hand down the length of Sellars, only stalling long enough to pop the button of her jeans and slide the zipper down, then she pushed her hand down inside.

"Don't close your eyes," Lacy whispered.

Sellars hummed as Lacy caressed her clit, dipping farther to tease her opening for several seconds, sliding easily through her wetness, before moving back to the spot, exactly where Sellars needed her to be.

For just a minute, she wanted Lacy to take her away from that haunting memory. The very one that darkened her mood far too often.

Lacy massaged in lazy circles and Sellars arched over her. Her eyes fluttered shut.

"Look at me!" Lacy said while she flicked faster.

Sellars opened her eyes to find Lacy staring at her. Pain and lust flickered in the depths of her eyes and she wondered if her own eyes mirrored the same thing.

"Just you and me, sexy." Lacy pressed her lips against Sellars's chest and inhaled. "No one else allowed."

Sellars stared down over her for several seconds, searching for malice, waiting for sarcasm, slowly circling her hips. When she found none, she palmed Lacy's face and pressed their lips together again.

She groaned against Lacy's mouth, grinding her hips in circles, until her orgasm ripped through her.

Lacy drove inside her, fisted her fingers into Sellars's hair, and swallowed her cries of release.

CHAPTER ELEVEN

Days had passed since Lacy cried out to an audience of pine trees with Sellars's face buried between her thighs.

Actually, she'd gone to great lengths to avoid her by burying herself in the so-called resurrection of Sellars's racing career. By spreading Sellars's pictures to several outlets of social media.

It had taken her a full day just to muster the courage to filter through the pictures she'd taken over the course of the last several days. Then more hours to bring her heart rate back down to a speed that wouldn't push her into cardiac arrest after going through the first lot of photos.

She repeated the process all day, alternating between posting and breathing.

Hot. Sellars was so fucking hot. And the pictures of her half-naked, shooting a bird at the world, her lips snarled back and angry, only fueled her sexual cravings.

Fuck. Too fucking hot.

After that, after having to choose which hot mess she needed to wing into cyberspace, she didn't have a choice but to dodge Sellars. She had to avoid that scent. Had to steer clear of the sight of her.

She was too weak not to.

If only she could stay out of her own head, like Sellars seemed to stay, where the most heated scenes appeared on their own accord. Out of the blue. Knotting her stomach.

Oh, how she wanted to do it all over again. This time, not with a cold hood beneath her. This time, without Sellars slipping away, without Lacy having to reel her back in.

Right now, she didn't trust herself not to repeat that mistake. Yes. It was a mistake. They had crossed a line and they couldn't go back. She knew the tension was going to be undeniable.

So, to avoid the walk of shame, she'd buried herself in social media, news feeds, spreading Sellars's "fuck you" pictures far and wide. From the feedback she was reading, they were working. People were loving how she was being herself, how she was telling everyone to kiss her ass with a single picture. Sure, there were still some hardcore haters, but she was starting to see some softness to a lot of the responses. Several threads had already begun to defend her, and Lacy couldn't help but smile.

Maybe she was going to pull this off after all. She had to. So many helpless people, homeless people, were depending on her to keep Sellars out of trouble so she could bring light to their world.

That alone left her full of excitement and eager to push forward, to take the next step with her head clear, full of positive thoughts, and the whip held tight in her grasp.

And that next step was soon. Like, in just a few hours. Sellars had a radio interview. She would be harassed and grilled by the haters and the lovers. Or so Lacy hoped there would be lovers.

Just one little break. That's all she needed. A window. A tiny opening in her otherwise doomed career. If she could just get that, Lacy was positive she could sail this ship all the way to the green flag where she'd drop Sellars off and be on her merry way.

With a sigh, she glanced back at the laptop. Sellars's photos were still open, dominating the screen with that angry glare.

Again, she wondered what dirty secrets rested inside that mind of hers. What had happened to the girlfriend? Did it matter? Days ago, it didn't. Now, a tiny part of her wanted to know.

She knew, whatever those secrets were, they were a direct link to her self-induced career suicide.

An hour later, she hesitantly stepped through the man cave door and found Sellars perched on a stool at the kitchen counter.

Goddamn. This was going to be a long day.

Sellars turned to look at her as she stepped through the basement door, and Lacy had a brief impulse to run back down the stairs.

She hadn't seen her face in two days. Had been hiding in that damn man cave to avoid this very reunion.

"You're alive!" Sellars leaned over the counter and set her empty cup in the sink. "I was beginning to wonder if your rotting corpse was going to stink up the house. Gabby would have had to use your swear jar cash for incense and aerosol sprays."

"Sorry to disappoint you. Gabby's college fund is safe and sound." Lacy continued across the room and headed for the front door, determined not to get too close to Sellars. She couldn't smell her. And for God's sake, she couldn't look at those eyes. "And social media is buzzing over your pictures. You may have a future after all despite your need to set it on fire. I know that disappoints you, too. Meet you in the car." She slipped out the front door without a glance and inhaled the fresh air, safe from her own dirty desires.

Sellars stared after her, wondering if Lacy had been avoiding her for a specific reason. A specific sexual reason. Did she regret their time together? Did she regret being weak? Being weak with Sellars?

There were a lot of things in her life she regretted, but sex with Lacy wasn't one of them and it made her uneasy to think that Lacy did.

And she was right. It was true. She'd sabotaged her own career. Why? Because she couldn't undo a past? Because she couldn't bring Sarah back? Because she was still pissed at her grandfather for buying her out of a deadly mistake?

For the first time in years, thoughts of Sarah hadn't plagued her all night. For the first time in years, her conscious was full of someone else.

They were now full of Lacy. She hated that. Because Lacy hated her. But it was peaceful to have freedom from herself. From her own hatred. From her regrets and guilt.

She had Lacy to thank for that even if she had just bee-lined past her without so much as a glance.

Self-medication. Isn't that what Lacy had said before?

Is that what Sellars was doing now? Feeding her guilt? Keeping it in motion? Keeping Sarah's memories alive in the process?

Was that such a bad thing, if so? To have feelings? To miss Sarah so bad it made her crazy? To have regrets eat her alive from the inside out?

No. It wasn't.

Forty-five minutes and a very quiet drive later, Lacy stood outside the glass enclosure at the radio station and watched

Sellars prepare for her radio interview. A woman fitted headphones on her while the radio host shuffled papers into order.

Lacy couldn't sit on the surrounding couches, too anxious for the questions from the callers to begin for Sellars. Most would be hostile. But hopefully, some wouldn't be. She needed Sellars to find some kind of confidence in herself. Some shred of proof that there were people out there who still liked her. Who wanted her on that track. Who didn't care if she was a bad girl with a need for speed.

They hadn't spoken a word on the drive over. All was eerily quiet while their little sexual secret lay wedged between them.

Even right now, with a thick pane of glass separating them, with Sellars just on the other side, it felt like she was worlds away. Out of reach.

But Lacy was a big girl wearing big girl panties. So was Sellars, as a matter of fact. They would continue this little business trip as if nothing ever happened.

The interview began.

Lacy listened through the speakers set in each corner of the room.

The "On Air" sign started blinking above the door.

"We have a special guest with us today." The DJ spoke into the microphone. "Kip Sellars. Newest rookie of NASCAR. Who has already made a name for herself climbing the ranks in Formula One in more ways than one."

He turned to Sellars with a chuckle. "I would love to talk about your bad girl reputation, but the phone lines are already lit up across the board here. I normally do a little meet and greet, but these people are beyond anxious to have a chat with you."

Sellars nodded. "By all means. Let's take a caller."

Lacy held her breath while the call was connected, secretly praying it would be a fan.

"Thank you for calling WXPT. Go ahead with your question."

"That bitch needs to get the hell out of NASCAR. She's not wanted here!" a male's voice bellowed through the speakers.

Lacy could only watch as Sellars gave a shrug and turned toward her own microphone. "Good thing you're not signing my paycheck."

The DJ cut the call and immediately picked up another.

"Hi! Thanks for calling WXPT. Did you have a question for Kip Sellars?"

"Oh my God!" a woman squealed. "Am I really on the air?"

"Yes, ma'am. Go ahead with your question."

"Sellars?" the woman cooed.

"Yes. I'm here. How are you?"

"Oh my Jesus. It's really you?" The woman started babbling while other voices filled the space behind her. "It's really her!"

"Ma'am, please go ahead with your question."

"I'll be at Sidewinders tonight! Come find me. Please please please. I'll be wearing your T-shirt!"

Sellars chuckled. "That sounds like a tasty invitation, but I'm banned from nightclubs until after the holidays, thanks to my own misbehavior." She lied. Sure, it was implied that she stay away but never placed in writing.

"Well, that sucks," the woman pouted. "Anywhere. You name the place. I'll be there!"

Sellars glanced toward Lacy. "Sorry, ma'am. They're making us move to another caller."

The DJ ended the call and poked Sellars's leg. "Wooowee! As you see, Pittsburgh, Sellars is a hot commodity."

Sellars pulled her sights away from Lacy while another caller was connected.

"Kip Sellars." A male voice filled the air. "How are you today?"

Sellars ground her teeth at the same time Lacy recognized the caller. Brett. That pissant just wouldn't go away. Then again, Sellars had screwed his wife. No doubt, that left a dirty little mark on their media perfect marriage.

Lacy held her breath while an evil grin passed over Sellars' lips.

"I'm doing great. How's that pretty wife? She still trying to teach an old, unsatisfying dog new, scream-inducing tricks?"

Lacy hung her head. Dammit, Sellars. Not good.

There was silence for several seconds before he chuckled. "Let's not waste air time on my life. Everyone, thanks to you, got to see all of it, up close and personal. That's old news now."

"True. But you have to admit, that wife of yours is very, very photogenic."

Lacy tapped the glass in warning. Sellars was goading the beast.

He took in a deep, calming breath. "This is your time, Sellars. This is your platform. Your pedestal. So, let's talk about *your* skeletons. Tell your new racing family how you murdered your girlfriend."

Lacy pecked the glass harder, but Sellars wouldn't look at her.

Sellars's jaw tightened as she moved closer to the microphone. "You're a dead man walking. Let's talk about *that*." She moved in closer, her lips almost brushing the foam cover, her teeth visibly clamped.

"We're all family here, Sellars," he said. "No need to be embarrassed. Although, I have to admit, I was a little embarrassed when I saw my wife making out with a nasty piece of murdering scum. But again, this isn't about me. Come on, tell us how it happened. Please, tell us how you killed her."

Lacy smacked her hands flat against the glass. The DJ turned to look at her, but Sellars was already gone. Her eyes narrowed on the microphone as if she could see down into it, find the fucker on the other side, and drag him through.

Sellars wrapped her hand around the stem of the microphone with a death grip. "I'm coming for you, buddy boy. And when I get to you, that little road rash you took on last year is going to feel like a Zip-a-Dee-Doo-Dah through the tulips."

Lacy slammed her hand against the glass again. Hard. The sound echoed back on her through the speakers.

She did it again as Sellars slid off the chair, hands planted on the desk, her mouth pressed against the foam.

"I'm going to—"

Lacy slapped her hands against the glass. Fast. Again. And again.

Her hands stung as she continued.

Finally, Sellars turned those hard eyes on her.

Lacy did the first thing that came to mind.

She grabbed the hem of her blouse, had one second to remember she wasn't wearing a bra, and then flashed Sellars.

The DJ spewed laughter.

Sellars stared at her breasts for several seconds, her gaze dancing from one to the other, before a smile lifted the corner of her lips, and she dropped back onto the stool.

Lacy lowered her shirt, her hands still shaking and stinging.

And suddenly, Sellars was laughing as well, and Lacy could see she was back down from her enraged high.

She leaned into the mic with casual ease. "Brett, slander can carry hefty fees and/or jail time. I'm going to let you slide this time, seeing as you're a recent divorcee. But I won't be so forgiving the next time. I'll see you on the track. In my rearview mirror." Sellars leaned back and the host disconnected the call.

Lacy breathed a sigh of relief while the DJ continued his interview. This time without callers.

This time with Sellars's penetrating eyes on her.

That wasn't the only thing Lacy wanted on her.

Thirty minutes later, they stepped out of the radio station into the brightness of the day.

"Have you ever ignored an asshole in your entire life?" Lacy said. "You need to practice some breathing techniques or counting or smoking or something. Damn."

Sellars turned and pasted a humorous stare on Lacy. "You worried about me?"

Lacy looked away, unable to peer into those eyes without images of her own hips rocking against Sellars's face filtering through her mind. "Hell no."

"Don't worry, sweetheart. Your paycheck is safe if that's what you're worried about."

Anger ripped through Lacy. She'd just flashed her tits for a whole room to see, simply to save Sellars from herself once again. "You think I'm trying to save your sorry ass for myself? No one in their right mind would sacrifice their own sanity to help a pathetic loser like you."

Lacy hated her words instantly. She didn't want to argue. Didn't want to yell or say things she couldn't take back. For once, she truly wanted to see Sellars succeed. Obviously, that was asking too much.

"Well, you got that right. No one in their *right* mind."
Sellars held her gaze on Lacy.

"Fuck you, Sellars."

"No thank you." Sellars stepped off the curb. "I'm not in the mood for paid sex today."

"You're a bitch," Lacy said, anger spiraling. Another emotion squeezed in. A feeling. She was pretty sure Sellars had just hurt her feelings, and she didn't like it one damn bit.

She darted off the curb behind Sellars and reached out to snatch the keys from her grasp. "I'm driving, loser!"

At the last second, Sellars jerked her hand away and cupped the keys in her fist. "My car. My keys. My turn. So get in the car or walk. The choice is up to you."

Sellars turned and plucked the driver's door open while Lacy stood dumbfounded.

No. She wasn't dumbfounded. She was horny. Being matched sure had its perks. If only they weren't in a parking lot with the whole world as their audience. If only Sellars hadn't just dared her.

She pounded to the passenger side and dropped into the seat. Anger and hot need whiplashed through her while Sellars fired the engine. This fucking bitch was going to grate her last nerve. Her very fucking last nerve.

Lacy folded those arms across her stomach and fumed. She was beyond pissed. She'd just made an idiot out of herself to save a jerk and yet she was still being accused of having ulterior motives.

Worse, she'd really wanted to drive. Drive and grind.

But not the car.

Dear Lord. Not the car.

CHAPTER TWELVE

Lacy growled under her breath as she scanned the length of tables set up along the center of the mall, finally spotting Sellars's table with its tiny little paper sign at least fifty feet away from the last table.

Who the fuck did these people think they were?

She'd expected Sellars to be at the last table. Would have expected nothing less considering she'd made herself an outcast who hadn't formed any type of bond with any of the other racers besides Billy, who wouldn't be attending today. Sellars was nobody to them. The baby of the family. The baby who had burned her bridges before she ever stepped foot on sacred ground.

But she hadn't expected the organizers to be a part of this ridiculous nonsense. For them to put her table so far from the rest. So far away that no one would have connected the fact that she was also here, in front of this sports store, as a part of that racing family, to sign autographs and sell her merchandise just like the rest of the racers would be doing.

"Oh, hell no. This is not happening." Lacy turned toward a group of racers who had formed a circle around one table, all gibbering and staring over their shoulder at her and Sellars.

"Don't worry about it," Sellars said. "I'd prefer to be apart from these jackasses."

"On the track, feel free to leave them in your dust trail," Lacy said, still feeling scorned from Sellars's hateful words yesterday. She wasn't used to having her feelings hurt. Hell, until those words had landed on her ears, she wasn't sure she had any feelings left. She was sorely proven wrong. Not that Sellars would ever know it. "But here, everyone will be treated with equal respect."

Before Sellars could stop her, Lacy stormed across the gap and grabbed the lone table. She hoisted one end in the air and started dragging.

The legs made a dramatic and teeth clenching screech that echoed along the still vacant hallway.

The chatter and laughter stopped as the racers turned toward the sound.

A woman holding a clipboard and nametag dangling around her neck, raced out of the sports store. "Ma'am!" She jogged toward Lacy who didn't break stride or even look at the woman. "You can't move the tables. They've all been positioned per a seating chart."

"What kind of seating arrangement puts one table out in the middle of Bumfuck, Egypt?" Lacy finally threw the woman a hostile glare while she continued dragging, stopping occasionally to get a different grip, maybe to give everyone hope that the sound had come to an end, before ripping away their hope only to begin again, amping up that nerve-grating noise until she had the table positioned exactly where she wanted.

Dead center of the square.

She dismissed the woman by walking around her. "The table stays right here, and I'm in a good damn mood for someone to try their luck with moving it." Lacy turned a daring stare on the woman.

"I'll send someone else out to speak with you." The woman took several steps back.

"Yes. Please do that. Scurry inside and let them know Kip Sellars has arrived and if anyone dares touch that fucking table, they'll be dealing with Mr. Reynolds personally."

The woman's mouth opened. She slipped her sights between Lacy and Sellars before pulling her precious clipboard to her chest. "Yes, ma'am. I'll bring out her boxes."

"Now we're on the same page." Lacy gave her a fake smile.

Sellars could only watch, her mind filling dangerously fast with all the tactful ways she could calm that trigger-happy attitude. How she could get under Lacy. How she wanted to get inside her. How she wanted to draw incoherent sounds from her mouth.

Yes. That's what she wanted. She wanted to make Lacy speechless. Again. And again.

No words. Just screams.

God only knew why. Lacy couldn't stand her. Even after their heated sexual moment, Lacy still thought of her as a loser. Had said as much. Had called her exactly that. She thought Sellars was going nowhere. That she was going to crash and burn long before her suspension was lifted.

Yet it hadn't stopped Lacy from demanding equality from this organization today. Demanding that she be treated with the same dignity and respect they were treating the rest of the racing pack.

What in the world for? Sellars didn't have any fans. Not a single person was going to request her John Hancock. She was an outcast. In her own family, and now in this racing family.

And she'd put herself here. With both families.

Sellars suddenly felt guilty for practically calling Lacy a hooker. Actually, she'd struggled with the need to march down those man cave stairs just to say the words. However, she was so turned on by the sight of Lacy's delicious nipples beyond the glass, hard and dark, haunting her thoughts into dirty images, that the words would have died on her lips right before Lacy came on them.

The woman came back out, ripping Sellars out of her heated thoughts, and politely set two boxes on the table. "Let me know if you need any help."

"You've helped quite enough, thank you." Lacy popped open a box and began organizing Sellars's memorabilia.

The woman glanced between them before walking away.

"I think you damaged her." Sellars chuckled.

"They shouldn't have sent a child to do a grown-up's job."

Lacy started pulling out the contents. Cups, mugs, T-shirts, keychains, photographs, and postcards.

All with her name. Her number.

Seeing this stuff, her dreams in living color, still made her giddy deep down inside.

She'd done it. She'd made it to a place that no one thought she could go. Conquered miles and miles of hell to reach this spot in time.

And here she was, dream tucked in her pocket, secure from anyone to take, standing here with a woman who thought she was trash, who she'd called a slut.

The emotion was rather comical. She'd felt empty the entire ride. So she'd filled that empty space with drama and sex and the party life, and created a rift, a wedge so wide she might never be able to cross back over, and she had no one to blame but herself.

A fact that Lacy was comfortable reminding her of quite often.

"Okay. You're all set up and I have some things to do," Lacy said.

"You're not staying?"

"Did you think I was going to sit here and hold your hand all day?"

"Well, no."

"Good because I'm not a hand-holder." Lacy tagged her in a dark stare. "Unless there was a bonus involved, since you seem to think I can be bought."

Ah. There it was. Lacy was still pissed about her heartless words.

As for hand-holding, she used to be into that. She rather liked holding hands with Sarah. Strolling. Dating.

She hadn't been on a date in so long, she wasn't sure she knew how to date anymore. Finding one-night stands came natural to her. Easy. And quick.

But never dates. Never ones she called back. If she even bothered to get their phone numbers at all. Most of the time she didn't. She had no plans to see them again. Not even for a second fuck.

She'd like to, though. Get a phone number. Go on a date. Stroll the many shops downtown. Go to a game. Eat ice cream. Have sex that didn't conclude after the orgasm.

"There you go drifting away again."

Sellars opened her mouth to apologize. Or so she thought those were the words she wanted to say.

"Don't. Don't you fucking dare say you're sorry," Lacy said.

Sellars closed her mouth but had every intention of showing Lacy that she regretted those words. There were better ways to say she was sorry. She'd start with her tongue.

"I'm out." Lacy glanced around, found another racer looking at their table, and gave him a daring raised eyebrow before he quickly turned away.

She turned back to Sellars, who looked absolutely delicious today in her dark jeans and pale gray blazer over that too tight T-shirt. Too many dirty thoughts had run through her mind in the past hour. Way too many to stick by Sellars's side all day while the fans ignored her completely. A problem she hoped to remedy before the day was over.

She didn't have to. She could snap a few boring pics to prove that Sellars had done the deed, but it grated her nerves to see so many judgmental people, so many who had been far worse, done far worse, who were judging Sellars for airing her dirty laundry without an apology.

"Sit there, don't move a fucking muscle, don't speak to a soul, and so help me God, if you misbehave, I will pay off your pit crew to disassemble your entire car on race day. Right down to the skinny frame. Every screw, every bolt, every hose and clamp. They all like me, so don't think for a second they won't."

Sellars could only grin. Lacy and her spitfire lips, made her horny as hell. How, she would never know. That tongue was razor sharp, and she meant every word that escaped that mouth.

She wanted to tame those lips. She wanted to make Lacy forget her next sentence. Wanted Lacy riding her face and screaming.

Damn. She wanted that scream so bad it made her squirm in her chair.

Lacy cocked an eyebrow. "I mean it. Don't fucking move."

She disappeared down the vacant hallway.

Thirty minutes slipped by after the doors were unlocked. Women and men crowded the other tables, begging for an autograph, women pleading for a selfie with their favorite racer.

But, as expected, no one approached her table. Not a single person took even a second glance in her direction. Most of the men scowled, but at least they kept their distance. Which was great because today was not a good day to go to jail.

Another thirty minutes went by, followed by a long hour. The crowd had now thickened, and she couldn't see anything beyond the line of people weaving around the tables.

This was such a waste of time. She could be working on her car. Taking a nap. Finding a bar for a few drinks.

Anything would do besides sitting here looking like an idiot. An outcast moron.

Then she heard someone shrill her name. Loud and penetrating.

And then it came yet again.

People turned toward the sound, some craning their heads to see over the line, all attention focused on the location of the voice.

And suddenly, Lacy pushed through the crowd. Her hair was down in long, sexy waves, and she was wearing a brand new pair of dark jeans rolled up around her ankles, a sheer overshirt that hung loosely around her body with her dark nipples pressed against the fabric. She was balancing herself on a pair of black spiked pumps. A pair of sunglasses that Sellars didn't remember her wearing on their way in, swept the mane of hair back from her face.

Numerous bags with different store logos dangled from her fingertips as she shoved through the last of the line.

"Kip Sellars!" Lacy squealed again. "Be still my heart, you're really here!"

She dropped the bags in front of the table and propped a hand up, dramatically pretending to catch her breath.

"I can't believe you are right here in front of me, in the flesh. All glorious inch of flesh. Jesus fucking Christ, I think I just came a little." She straightened and pretended a little gasp. "I'm so sorry. I'm showing my bad girl true colors. Wherever are my manners? I'm Lacy. My daddy is here on business, and I came to keep him company, but those business meetings were hideous so he gave me his credit card and waved me away. As if tearing up the mall was a punishment." She winked.

Lacy thrust her hand out to Sellars. "It's so great to meet you, Sellars. I've been following your career for so many years. You're incredible!"

Sellars slowly took her hand, wondering what kind of game she was playing or exactly how to play along with the charade. "Thank you."

Lacy flipped her long hair over a shoulder. "My daddy is your biggest fan. Said you were the hottest thing to hit the track." She fanned her fingers across her neck like she was wiping away sweat that didn't exist. "He was referring to your speed and agility and determination to win those races." She leaned down but didn't lower her voice. "But goddamn, you're the hottest thing I've ever laid eyes on. Those filthy, lying tabloids did no justice at all showing just how delicious and chewy and edible you truly are. My good God Almighty, can I take you home to our ranch, darling?"

Sellars could only arch a brow, too amused to respond. Her insides clenching too tight to move.

"Oh my goodness. There goes my manners again. I'm acting like a horny teenager pining for her first piece of ass."

Lacy bent down, exposing her cleavage to the audience around her, and dug into one of the bags. "If you could be so kind, my entire family would kill me if I didn't get your autograph."

Lacy slapped a stack of eight-by-ten photographs on the table and Sellars drew in a shocked gasp.

Her fuck off picture. Her lips snarled back, middle fingers to the world.

Lacy had taken them minutes before Sellars had tasted her.

"I need one for my daddy. His name is Carl, by the way." Lacy rushed on. "He's your biggest fan. Did I say that? And one for my Papa Jeff. But please sign that Jethro because that's what his racing game day buddies call him. They all pile up at the country club to watch you. Bless their hearts. They're so stinking cute." She stalled long enough to pull air into her lungs. "My sister, Sheila, and her husband, Grant. My brother Richard and his wife, Patty. And my…. Oh Lord, you're so damn hot I've plum forgot the most important person."

Lacy leaned over the table, pushing her ass out to the crowd behind her. "Me. I want your autograph on me. Right here." She pulled the sheer fabric of her shirt apart.

Sellars had no choice but to look down. No bra. Just naked skin teasing her with how much more she wanted to see. How much more she wanted to taste and chew.

"Can you do that for me, sexy?" Lacy whispered.

Sellars picked up the unused permanent marker lying by her fingers and rose from the chair. She couldn't drag her gaze from Lacy's chest. The images of Lacy lying flat on her back against the hood flooded her conscious. She wanted to do that again. Needed to do that again.

She ripped off the cap, leaned into Lacy, and signed her name.

"Thank you," Lacy whispered again.

Her sights slipped down to Sellars's lips for several seconds before she blinked and stood up. She picked up one of the photos and waved it above her head. "Ladies! I made extras of this hot piece of ass! Grab them before they're all gone!"

One by one, people moved toward her table.

Before Sellars knew it, the mall was closing.

She'd sold every hat and keychain, every T-shirt and postcard, and signed more skin than should be humanly possible.

She spotted Lacy across the aisle sitting on a bench, a pleased expression on her face.

Lacy had done that for her. She truly couldn't stand Sellars, she'd been called a whore, yet she'd made a spectacle of herself to draw in a crowd. Was the money that important that there was no level she wouldn't stoop to? Or was she witnessing Lacy's true colors? Her loyal, treat everyone equal, colors?

Did Sellars even care?

In a single day, in a single squeal, Lacy had managed to win back the possibility of a fan base. Her very own fan base. For that, Sellars couldn't thank her enough.

Lacy finally wandered over behind the table with Sellars, a smile teetering on her lips. "Was that fun for you?"

Actually, it had been. She felt adored, wanted, and admired. The crowd had made her feel included instead of an outcast.

"Well, look what the hell the cat dragged in," a man announced as he approached the table, interrupting the thank you from her lips. "Lacy. Lacy. Lacy. How the hell are you doing, stranger?"

Lacy grumbled under her breath. "I was perfect until I heard that grating voice, Leonard." She stood tall to face him.

"Still got that cutthroat attitude, I see." Leonard took another step forward, and Sellars felt her guard go up.

"Why change when I'm perfect just the way I am?" Lacy said.

"Oh, you changed all right. Change didn't seem to bother you when you tucked that tail between your legs and ran like a coward." Leonard lifted his chin in defiance. "Tried to tell you this was a man's world and women didn't belong here."

"Women belong everywhere, assface."

"Coming from a woman who sold her soul to the devil, I'll pass on Righteous Lesson 101."

Lacy charged, startling Sellars out of her inspection of the man. "You piece of shit, ass licker. You don't know what the fuck you're talking about!" She pushed the table to the side like child's play and barreled for him.

He jumped back.

Sellars leapt forward and grabbed Lacy around the waist, pulling her back just as Lacy reached out for him.

Leonard stepped farther back. "Holy shit, wildcat. Is that any way to treat an old friend?"

Lacy pushed against Sellars's arm, her legs kicking, her lips curled back in a snarl. "I'm going to claw your fucking eyes out, you garbage disposal!"

To Sellars's disbelief, several racers ran toward them.

Lacy twisted in Sellars's grasp. "Let me punch his fucking lights out." She kicked out. "He's a lying piece of scum, fucking shit face, goddamn troublemaking coward."

Spittle flew from her mouth, and Sellars dragged her back several feet.

"Leonard, I think it's time for you to go." Stephen, one of the racers, stepped in between.

"Hey, man. I was just here to snap a few shots for the tabloids." Leonard held up his hand defensively.

"Why?" Lacy bellowed. "So you can shovel a pile of repulsive lies in them? Like you always do!" She shoved against Sellars again. "Take my fucking picture now, you lowlife piece of cow dung. I got the perfect tagline for you! Karma reaps revenge on worthless, lowlife reporter."

Stephen turned toward Sellars. "Get her out of here before she kills his sorry ass." He turned back to Leonard with a glare. "You! Start walking!"

Sellars tightened her grip around Lacy's waist and ducked out the double doors that led into the courtyard. She didn't loosen her grip until they were in the parking lot beside her car and she felt safe she could catch Lacy if she fled back to finish what she so desperately wanted to start.

Lacy jerked out of her grasp and started pacing. "I hate that man. He's a worthless...a worthless..." She stomped along the side of the car. "I hate him. One day. One fucking day."

The woman with her clipboard raced across the parking lot with Lacy's bags dangling from her hands. "Ma'am! You left your bags!"

She came to a breathless stop, and with a forlorn expression, she held the bags out to Lacy. "I'm sorry about earlier."

Sellars held her breath while Lacy calmly took the bags, terrified she'd use this woman as her personal punching bag.

As soon as the bags were out of her grasp, the woman turned and jogged back across the parking lot.

Sellars took the bags from her and dropped them into the back seat.

Lacy looked up at Sellars, tears of anger glistening in her eyes, her small hands tightened into a fist. "Get me out of here before I change my mind and go back for blood. I'm beyond irrational."

Sellars reached around her and opened the car door. "Get in."

Lacy ducked inside, her sights trained on the windshield.

Sellars closed the door with only one destination in mind.

It was time to tame the tiger.

Again.

CHAPTER THIRTEEN

Lacy fumed as Sellars drove them through the city; this time she was actually five miles over the speed limit. She'd even changed lanes more than a few times to move around slower drivers.

She wanted to compliment her, to tell her it was about damn time she drove like a race car driver, that she was driving like a normal Pittsburgher, but she was still too pissed to utter a word.

Leonard and his tacky lies. He was right about one thing. He was the true reason she packed her shit and left this beautiful city. The reason she had left Billy and his family. He and his colleagues who never hesitated to spread exactly what they wanted, no matter how many lives they damaged, no matter how many lives those lies affected.

He was a true piece of shit, and one day karma was going to find him. Lacy prayed she'd get to watch. Better, she hoped karma would let her land one single punch before she took over. Maybe two. No. Three. One for Doug. One for his family. And the final, for Lacy. She deserved all three.

Sellars pulled up to a gate, punched in a code, then pulled through. The decorative metal silently closed behind them.

Inside the condo complex was a paradise. Evergreens littered the bright green grounds in various shapes and sizes and the grass was so green Lacy had to resist the urge to make Sellars stop the car so she could walk barefoot through it. She'd never seen anything this close to the East Coast look so much like the West Coast. Bright and cheery and so green. It was remarkable, and she couldn't take it all in fast enough as Sellars moved swiftly along the street.

"Where are we?"

Sellars pulled into a vacant spot and got out. "This isn't a date, so open your own door."

Lacy obeyed, inhaling the scent around her. She couldn't imagine what the air would smell like with all the trees in bloom. When they bloomed. "Did we just warp into another dimension? How do they keep these trees so beautiful with all the ice and snow?"

Sellars paced down a walkway that led to a wooden gate like a woman on a mission. "I've never asked. And I won't start today." She lifted the lock and pushed open the door to reveal a small patio area, free of plants or chairs or anything that proved someone lived there. Beyond that was a sliding glass door.

Lacy followed and waited while she unlocked the door.

Sellars slid the glass open, moved back, and waved Lacy through, her face unreadable.

"Is this your new apartment? I thought it was being renovated."

"Stop talking, Lacy."

Lacy took in her serious expression. Her insides tightened, and suddenly, she wasn't so mad anymore. Actually, the anger had simmered down as soon as she spotted a tropical oasis in the middle of what would soon be a white world. It was one of the things she missed most about Pittsburgh. The snow. Months of it. The mountains and riverbanks were magnificent blanketed in white.

The memory of snuggling down in a blanket to watch the snow fall, flooded her mind. How she wished she'd never left. How she wished she'd held her head high, tucked down her fear, pushed down her need to spit in Leonard's face, and stayed right where she was.

But that career crashed and burned with Doug's death. She could never be that same person she was then. That fearless person. That person hopelessly devoted to Billy.

No matter how much time passed, she could never go back to that old career. It warmed her heart to know that she no longer wanted to.

The door clicked behind her, pulling Lacy out of her moment.

"Keep walking," Sellars said.

If the command hadn't sounded so sexual, she'd disobey, deliberately, loudly, blasting Sellars with nonstop chatter.

But that scolding expression told Lacy that she should obey. This time. She turned toward the living area so she wouldn't catch a glimpse of the lust in Sellars's eyes anymore. She would fall into them otherwise.

There was no furniture. Not even a picture on any of the walls as she took another step, obeying.

The whole place was vacant.

Footsteps sounded behind her. Lacy's heart hammered, and her insides tightened as she turned around to find Sellars inches away, staring down over her.

Those eyes. Those damn eyes.

Sellars pushed herself against Lacy and claimed her lips.

Lacy hummed as Sellars urged her lips apart with the tip of her tongue. Fire shot down her chest and curled tight in her crotch.

Sellars groaned and the sound galvanized Lacy. She snaked her arm around Sellars's neck and wove her fingers into her hair, then pressed harder into that tight body.

She shouldn't be here. Shouldn't be alone with Sellars. She knew it, yet she couldn't stop herself. Wouldn't stop herself. Didn't want to stop herself.

Sellars palmed her ass and smoothly pulled Lacy's legs up and around her hips.

She walked gracefully through the living area and into the bedroom, her hands squeezing Lacy's ass, her mouth demanding, devouring, and then she dropped Lacy onto a bed.

Without giving Lacy any time to object, Sellars ripped off her tennis shoes, overwhelmed with the need to feel those releasing spasms around her fingers, against her tongue. She'd never been so consumed with such an aching need so bad. The desire was blinding. The thirst was unbearable.

She tugged off Lacy's pumps, too impatient for those lips again to rip off the rest of her clothing, then she crawled over her. With a growl, she took possession of Lacy's lips again, driving her hips forward, groaning against Lacy's mouth.

Now, she needed to be inside her. Right now, she needed to hear that cry of release. The need was too strong. God, it was so strong.

Lacy grabbed her ass and forced her to drive again.

Sellars obliged, pumping into her, swallowing Lacy's sharp gasps.

Even the sound of her was addicting. She needed more of that. More of those sexual sighs. More of those eager moans.

But more than all of the above, she needed to feel her skin against Lacy's. Needed the taste of Lacy on her lips. The tone of her release against her ears.

Like nothing else she ever needed in her life, she needed to get inside this woman.

Lacy bucked up to meet her thrusts, tugging at Sellars's jacket.

Yes. Sellars needed this jacket off. These clothes. She leaned back on her heels, tugged the blazer off, shucked the T-shirt over her head, and fell back over Lacy, promptly capturing those lips again.

They were like a drug. Plump and kissable, and right now, they were silent.

She liked that more than anything. Lacy's tongue free of poison.

Lacy locked her legs around Sellars's hips and dragged her nails down her back.

The sweet sting of pain settled in, and Sellars instinctively bucked into her again.

Lacy couldn't stand her. Possibly hated her. Yet Sellars couldn't get enough of her. She'd never wanted anything to do with anyone who showed their intolerance of her. But Lacy was different. Somehow, her blatant dislike wasn't like a knife in her back. It was like a stimulant.

Right now, she couldn't fucking get enough. As Lacy would say.

She grabbed Sellars's ass and drove her hips forward, begging with her actions for more. More. More.

Sellars pushed her hands between them, her lips still hard against Lacy's, and ripped at her jeans.

Desperate to help, desperate for her weight, more desperate for penetration and skin, Lacy shoved her hands between them and desperately tugged at Sellars's jeans. The button finally disengaged.

Hopeless to be inside Sellars, for Sellars to be inside her, Lacy used her hands, her knees, then her feet, to work Sellars's jeans down her thighs.

Sellars finally pulled back and wrestled their jeans down and off while Lacy slipped out of her blouse.

When Sellars looked back down over her, lust danced in those eyes as she looked from one nipple to another. Lacy had never felt so treasured. So cherished. Or so wanted.

Sellars was spiraling out of control. She was going down in flames. It was just a matter of time. Yet, right here, right now, all Lacy saw was a woman who was broken, who had deliberately hidden all of the pieces so that no one could put her back together.

Thankfully, Lacy had no desire to be the glue.

She leaned up, wrapped her arms around Sellars's neck, and pulled her back down.

Finally, skin against skin.

Sellars claimed her lips once again and Lacy hummed against her mouth. For once, for the first time since Sellars's looked up in the detention center parking lot, Lacy didn't despise her.

She wanted her. If only for a little while.

Sellars pushed her hand between them, then lifted her head to watch Lacy. She teased Lacy's slick opening, her gaze curious and dark, her lips parted as she stared down at Lacy.

Before Lacy could beg her for penetration, Sellars pushed inside her. Slow and deliberate.

Lacy arched off the bed while the sensations overwhelmed her, while her insides tightened around those fingers.

Sellars pulled out and drove back in, until Lacy was wrapped around her, bucking, her orgasm scrambling to the surface so fast it made her dizzy.

Her insides clamped down in warning, and then she came in a blinding rush of electric energy.

She screamed and thrashed under Sellars's weight, grinding her hips, clawing at the bare skin beneath her fingertips.

And finally, she sagged against the mattress.

Sellars rolled onto her side, and Lacy could feel her staring.

She didn't want to talk. Didn't want to move. Didn't want to fucking think about what they were doing. What they had done again. The thing Lacy swore would never happen again.

Yet, here she was, once more, because she was a pathetic weak ass.

"What?" Lacy grunted.

"Tell me about Leonard."

Lacy opened her eyes to look at her. "You sure know how to ruin a mood."

"Call it intermission." Sellars grinned. "Spill it."

Lacy focused on her surroundings for the first time. No dresser. No clothes in the open closet. Just a bed.

"Please tell me this isn't your fuck palace." Lacy wasn't so sure it would matter at this point. She couldn't have stopped herself to save her own sanity.

"You'll be happy to know you're the first to come in this apartment." She winked, and Lacy resisted the urge to crawl over her, grind her hips against that fit body until another orgasm robbed her of the need to truly spill it.

She didn't like talking about Leonard. Or the death she captured during routine practice. A place she wouldn't have been if she hadn't wanted to flirt with one of the pit crew. A woman recently employed by another racer's team.

Yet, there she'd been, happy to be in Billy's world, striking up the "we're going to fuck later" conversation with the new hottie, and trying out her brand new camera.

And if those things hadn't been worse, she'd walked down the hill just to get the best view of the curve. The place was empty save for a few wives or girlfriends and track personnel.

She hated that she'd been bored all day. That she'd needed to get laid. That she'd gone there to do just that.

The practice had been simple. Around the track they'd gone. Simple. Just simple circles. Not too much speed. Warming up the tires, she'd heard Doug say before.

And then he'd increased the speed. Climbing high in the curves. Dipping low. Warming up those damn tires.

Lacy had captured it all, excited at how vivid the images appeared. Normally, she didn't spend a tiny fortune on a camera. But this one had called her name. Had been light in her grasp.

Doug was on the long stretch. She could hear his engine whining as he increased the speed. And suddenly, he slammed the brakes, which immediately sent him into a spin.

The tires caught on the pavement and then he was airborne.

Every flip of that car, every shattered piece of metal, every inch of his body ejecting through the windshield, she'd captured.

Lacy swallowed. "He's an ass face who triggered a story about me after Doug's family started the lawsuit against NASCAR."

"That you sold the photos to Doug's family?" Sellars shifted closer to Lacy's side.

"Yes."

"Did you?"

Lacy turned to look at her. Her heart rate quickened until she saw the lack of malice in Sellars's eyes. "No. Of course not."

"Then how did they get the photos?"

"Me. I gave them every single one."

"So they could go after NASCAR?"

Lacy shook her head. "No." She turned her gaze on the ceiling. "I couldn't keep them. Couldn't look at them. But I couldn't delete them, either."

"That must have been hard," Sellars whispered. "Witnessing that. Capturing that."

Lacy felt her throat tighten with the sound of pity. She didn't want Sellars's pity. Not anyone's, as a matter of fact.

"Lisa had a case. I had the proof. It was the right thing to do." Lacy rolled onto her side to face Sellars, eager for this conversation to be over, eager to get back to the place where they were too breathless to speak.

"So you gave them the ammunition and hightailed it across the map? Did you think NASCAR was going to put out a contract for your head? I don't think it works that way."

Lacy considered her question. She hadn't run from NASCAR. That lawsuit would have come at them regardless of Lacy's photos. Even they knew that. They'd settled so fast, it never had a chance to enter a courtroom, and the seat belts had been changed in every car as a result.

No. She'd run from her own demons. The demons those pictures created. The demons Leonard created with his filthy lies.

Fact was, she was terrified it would happen again. Terrified the next person would be Billy.

"Leonard's right. I was in a man's world. I didn't belong there. I'm not cut out to be a groupie. Or a NASCAR photographer." Lacy fingered Sellars's arm, anxious to shut those lips, to shut out the images that were starting to nudge at her conscious.

"Bullshit," Sellars said. "He was just trying to get in your head." She cupped Lacy's wrist. "And you'd never let a man run you off. He wasn't the reason."

Sellars rolled Lacy onto her back and settled between her thighs once again. "What were you running from, Lacy?"

"Shut up and fuck me."

Sellars smiled while she hooked Lacy's legs over her hips. She slowly arched into her.

Lacy pushed her hand down the length of her body until she found Sellars's slick opening. She teased for several seconds, watching Sellars's smirk melt from her face.

She drew her fingers back up and slowly circled her clit.

"Finally. I didn't think you were ever going to shut up." Sellars lowered herself over Lacy, slipped her own hand between Lacy's thighs, and pushed inside her.

Together, they fucked each other, panting, crying out, until they both fell beside each other in a sweaty heap.

What felt like eternity slipped by while Lacy surrendered to the tranquil moment. Normally, she'd be dressed by now. Normally, she would be headed for the door.

But nothing was normal lately.

And right now, this was perfectly abnormal.

Even when Sellars moved, she wanted to stop her. She needed a few more minutes of this. This, nothing. Just lying there, thinking about nothing. Doing nothing. She never did nothing enough. Always on the go. Always working on something. Always.

"Get dressed. I have a surprise for you." Sellars bent over the bed and started chucking clothes at Lacy.

"I don't like surprises," Lacy said as she sorted through the clothing for her shirt and pants.

She didn't like surprises because she never got them.

Unless it came in the mail from Billy or Gabby, surprises didn't land at her feet.

"Do you trust me?" Sellars stuffed her legs into her jeans.

"Hell no. Why would I trust a death wisher?" Lacy buttoned the shirt into place.

When she looked up, Sellars was staring down over her.

That look of need in her eyes was all Lacy could handle.

She reached out and pulled Sellars back down.

Whatever the surprise was, it would have to wait.

CHAPTER FOURTEEN

When Sellars turned onto the no outlet street, Lacy knew immediately where they were going.

The racing school.

She could feel her anxiety settling in for the long haul.

She tried to calm her knotting stomach, repeating to herself that the school was closed this hour of the night, that no one would be on the track, that it was okay.

She hadn't been to a track—any track—since the day of Doug's fatal wreck. Not even to watch Billy. Not even when the crew threw him a birthday party from the pit. Never.

"Why the fuck are we here?" Lacy could hear the tremble in her voice, and the sound aggravated her.

She didn't like being a damsel. Didn't like appearing weak.

"Helping." Sellars parked the car and jumped out. She came around to Lacy's door.

Lacy shoved the door open. "We're still not on a date. I'll open my own damn door." She stepped out and glanced at the building. "How is standing in a parking lot of a racing school in the middle of the night helping? Helping with what, is the better question."

Sellars withdrew her cell phone, sent what Lacy assumed was a text, then took Lacy's hand. "Come on. You won't regret it. I promise."

Sellars pulled her forward and Lacy prayed she meant those words.

She fought to put every foot in front of each other. Sellars's hand felt so good in hers, and that was the only reason she kept taking the steps that were leading her closer and closer to that racetrack. To that evil death track.

She hated her fear more than anything. This, a track, the adrenaline of the race, was where she'd always felt the most confident in her photography. The men behind the scenes. The racers themselves. They'd always made her feel like family.

Until that day.

No matter how many pep talks she had in silence with herself, no matter how many times she reminded herself that when your time was up, then time was simply up, no matter where you were. She could never talk herself out of allowing the fear to eat her alive from the inside out.

Worse were the memories. The images she could never shake from her mind. They would forever be ingrained.

A young man wearing wire-rimmed glasses and a flop haircut appeared at the entrance. He pushed the door open with a smile and motioned for them to come inside.

Lacy hesitated. She wasn't sure why. It was the middle of the night. There wouldn't be cars on the track, nor could she hear that enticing roar.

But she was close. Close to a track that had claimed a life. A life she'd captured until his last breath.

Sellars squeezed her hand, and the pressure reminded Lacy that she was showing her weakness again.

She stepped inside.

The walls were full of photographs. Big names. Like Richard and Dale and David. The greats, as they would always be referred to.

She tried to concentrate on them instead of looking through the opposite wall of glass. The glass that looked out over the track. The very one she'd been looking through the day of Doug's death. The fucking one she couldn't get a good enough view through.

With a swallow, Lacy turned to another wall, desperate not to even let the glass move into her peripheral vision.

"Jared is our little secret." Sellars interrupted her mental anguish. "He lets me come here at night. To practice."

Lacy finally turned to look at her, praying that anguish wasn't written all over her face. The last person she wanted to feel sorry for her was Sellars. "You're not allowed anywhere near a track during your suspension."

Sellars stepped into her, and Lacy felt the needles of doubt ease. "I won't tell if you don't."

Lacy glanced over Sellars's shoulder to find Jared grinning at them. She stepped back. "Don't be so dramatic. I couldn't give a shit if you drive headfirst into your own demise. It's obvious by your track record, on and off that oval ring, that you're a big girl making little girl decisions. Now, again, what are we doing here?"

Sellars gave her that signature smile and pointed toward the stairwell. "After you, princess."

Lacy wanted to be brave, but that little voice in her head screamed that this was a very bad idea, that if they got caught, it was all over for Sellars. And if she got too close to that death track, it would be all over for her as well. She wasn't so sure her heart could take the steady palpitations already making a hardy rhythm in her chest.

Memories threatened, and she lifted her chin, defying their entrance.

She started walking. Down the circular stairwell to the bottom floor where the wall of glass felt like a panel of death.

That voice was screaming as she strode to the double doors that led outside, no doubt the direction they were headed.

What the hell was Sellars up to? And why?

What purpose did this trip serve?

She shoved open the doors and drew in a deep breath, aware that Sellars was close on her heels.

Another set of stairs led down to the edge of the track where Lacy spotted a race car. She stopped cold.

"We're not getting in that car."

Sellars stopped beside her, unsure if this was such a good idea after all. Lacy might sound normal, minus the catch in her voice, but she was anything but normal. Her eyes were darting around like she expected danger to appear out of thin air. Sellars felt like a total shit for bringing Lacy back to the scene of the crime.

This was where Sellars came to help fight those demons. Or rather, in her case, entice them to the surface.

But it had seemed like a logical idea. Logical self-medication, as Lacy had said.

Right now, she was second-guessing her own intentions with that look of helplessness in Lacy's eyes, no matter how hard she was trying to hide it. This was anything but a good idea.

Maybe she should take Lacy and her sarcastic devil tongue back to her apartment before those verbal slaps in the face gave her whiplash.

"You're right. We're not. You and Jared are."

Sellars almost stepped back when Lacy turned a glare on her.

"I will do no such fucking thing." Lacy shook her head, her gaze returning to the car at the edge of the track.

Sellars resisted the urge to hug her. Not only would that dog bite, she'd chew her up and leave unidentifiable body parts in the aftermath.

But one thing was for sure. Lacy was terrified of this place. It was written all over her expression. Those demons were on her back.

Was it wrong for Sellars to want to help her shake them? Was it wrong to think this was the place to do it? Was it wrong to get involved at all? To care?

Of course it was. Lacy was only here for the paycheck at the end of the ride. She was only here because, once again, her grandfather was paying Sellars's way out of her own mess.

But something deep inside pulled at her, telling her that Lacy needed this moment far more than Sellars needed to come clean about her past.

For some reason, that made her feel good about herself. That if for nothing else, she would have done a good deed for someone other than herself.

"Yes, you will because you know I'm right."

Lacy continued to stare at the car and Sellars wondered what she was thinking. Was she considering the fact that Sellars was right? Did Sellars's presence make her more comfortable? Because Sellars carried her own demons, even if Lacy didn't know the details?

"Then you drive." Lacy turned around and pasted an "I dare you" expression on her face.

Sellars gave a nervous chuckle, hearing her own fear in the sound. "Jared is the pro here. Not me."

She hadn't had a woman in the passenger seat of a car that was doing over freeway speed limits since Sarah's death. Since she opened her eyes to a film of blood and the love of her soul lifeless across the hood.

For a second, she closed her eyes against the images only to realize they were fresher with her eyes closed.

"You drive or take me home. The choice is yours, and it's the only choice you have." Lacy lifted her chin.

Sellars stared at that stern expression, those eyes serious and daring, searching for the bluff. She didn't find one.

"Make up your mind. I don't have all night." Lacy turned and started down the steps as if she knew, or hoped, Sellars would fall for the challenge and follow her. "Or maybe I'll just drive the damn thing myself. I'm not afraid of the car, idiot."

Sellars drew in a deep breath, watching Lacy retreat even farther down the stairs, already feeling the weight of emotions dragging her down. "I can't, Lacy. Let's just call it a night."

Lacy stopped and turned to look at her. "Bullshit, you can't. You dragged me here in the middle of the night, tell me to face my fear, and you can't even take the wheel? Sounds like a coward to me. A hypocritical coward."

Lacy was right. Sellars hated that more than anything. That the tables were being turned. That the good of the night had turned on its head, forcing her into her own regression. Forcing her to face her own demon face-first.

With a grunt, she stormed down the stairs. She could do this. It was just a car. It was just a woman in the passenger seat. No harm. No foul.

Yes. She could do this.

Lacy watched Sellars jerk the suit off the hood of the car. She kicked off her shoes and stepped into the coveralls while Jared helped Lacy with her own.

She wouldn't even look at Lacy, and her expression was unreadable.

Was she realizing what a waste of time this trip was? Did she want to take Lacy's hand and U-turn them back up those stairs, back through the building, and get the hell out of here?

Who the hell did she think she was? She wanted to heal Lacy with a rip around the track but wouldn't answer even the smallest question about her own past?

Fact was, she wasn't going to open up. She'd made that clear. And the fact that she thought she could bring Lacy here and heal her with speed medication was a joke.

Was she pissed that she didn't win this argument? That Lacy was forcing her to help smash the demons? Mad because Lacy would prefer she take her around this track? Would it make her feel better to know that out of the two people here, maybe out of a dozen racers, Billy not included, she trusted Sellars the most?

She was an amazing driver, smooth and graceful, and she didn't risk safety on the track. She was one hell of a driver and Lacy trusted her. Completely.

But there was something deeper. Something that meant even more than her ability to control a race car. Lacy somehow knew Sellars would never cause her harm.

She trusted her. And that trust didn't come easy.

A fact she would keep to herself for now. Sellars had a big enough head as it was.

Sellars yanked the zipper closed. "Let's get this over with." She dodged around to the driver's side, lifted her legs over the frame, and dropped into the seat like a pro.

It was rather sexy. She was sexy. Another fact Lacy needed to keep to herself.

Lacy climbed through the door. Not as gracefully as Sellars.

She dropped into the seat and anxiousness overwhelmed her.

Fear. Excitement. Adrenaline. The combination balled in her gut, but she refused to give in to the demanding need to escape.

Sellars was right. It was time to do this. Time to face her fear. Time to circle this track. If for nothing, she'd do it for Doug. She'd do it for his family who had easily won their case with Lacy's photos. Changes were made. Racers were safer because of her bravery. Lives would be saved because Lacy was in the wrong place at the wrong time, doing nothing more than looking for a fuck and taking a new camera for a spin.

Jared reached in and pushed the helmet over Lacy's head, buckled it under her chin, then snapped the seat belt into place. "Have fun!"

He backed away from the car, and Lacy had the urge to jerk at the tightness. Claustrophobia nipped at her mind, and she lightly inhaled to fight the emotion.

Sellars worked her own helmet into place and fired up the engine. The car rumbled beneath them.

The vibration soothed Lacy somehow.

Now. She needed Sellars to drive now, before she changed her mind. Before she ran screaming from this pit of despair.

Sellars reached over and jerked on Lacy's seat belt. Then again.

Lacy pushed her hand away. "Put your fucking foot on that pedal!"

Sellars felt like the oxygen had been pulled out of the air. Lacy was in the seat beside her. Not Sarah. She was on a racetrack. Not a back road. The only thing that could possibly jump out in front of her this time was air.

She said that to herself again as she pushed in the clutch. Once again as she pushed the gear into position. And finally, once again, as she pulled away from the curb.

Her chest tightened as they exited the pit area and merged onto the track.

She could do this. She could. She was no longer that punk high schooler simply racing for the fun of it. She was no longer that arrogant dumbass who thought no harm could come her way.

It could. It had. And it had cost her the most precious thing in her life.

Lacy wasn't Sarah. This wasn't a slick ride where she got to fuck in the back seat by the end of the night.

She was a professional racer. She had won many races. She had dominated.

She was damn good at racing. She owned the speed. She owned the car and every maneuver. She was a badass. She was born to control a car.

So why didn't she feel more confident? Why did she feel like a weight was pinned against her chest?

"For the fucking love of puppies, are you going to creep around this track too?" Lacy barked. "Do I look like a goddamn damsel? Punch this bitch."

The weight pushed even harder with Lacy's demand.

How had the tables been turned? How was she the one on the verge of hyperventilating when this trip was to help Lacy chase her demons away?

How the hell had Lacy managed to turn the table on her?

"Do it, Sellars!"

Sellars pushed the pedal harder, increasing the speed past her comfort zone. Actually, Lacy being in this car at all was beyond her cushion of comfort.

People died when they sat in that seat. When her foot was on the floor. When her car was cutting through air.

"Yes!" Lacy hissed.

Sixty. Seventy.

The memories nudged at her conscience, and she struggled to keep them at bay. Normally, she would welcome Sarah's memory. Normally, the speed pulled them to the surface. Normally, she wanted them there. Wanted Sarah's image alive and by her side.

Normally.

Not today. Not now. Not with Lacy in that space beside her, encouraging her to go faster.

Not when she was mentally fist fighting to hold on to her sanity.

Eighty. Ninety.

The images pushed harder. Pushing. Shoving at her conscience to be set free.

She gripped the steering wheel like her life depended on it. No. Like Lacy's depended on it. Because her life did depend on Sellars's ability to not make a mistake. A mistake she'd already made once.

Lacy squealed as Sellars rose higher on the track.

The sound yanked at her. Her heart squeezed into a painful vice.

She squeezed the steering wheel even tighter as she struggled not to let those memories take control.

And then those images crashed through. Pummeling through her mind as they always did when the needle climbed.

Sarah squealing from the seat beside her. The trees zooming alongside them. The speed beneath them. Her arms through that sunroof, demanding that Sellars go faster. Faster. Faster.

"Go faster, Sellars!" Lacy shrieked.

The sound of her voice sliced through, and Sellars couldn't breathe. The weight was too much.

She cut down the embankment, shot onto pit road, and slammed on the brakes. They slid several yards, tires screaming beneath them, and finally, the car jerked to a stop.

"Get out!" Sellars said. "Get out of the car."

"What the fuck?" Lacy tugged the helmet off her head.

Sellars removed her own helmet but couldn't, or wouldn't, look at Lacy. "Just get out. Please."

Lacy took in her expression. Set and determined. Sadness lay behind her downward cast eyes. The car. The speed. The track. She wasn't sure which had triggered Sellars into this mood, but for sure, it was one of the above.

"Does this have something to do with your girlfriend?" Lacy asked.

Sellars looked out the window and her jaw clenched.

"Tell me what happened, Sellars." Lacy tugged at the seat belt.

Sellars continued staring out the window.

"Talk to me, dammit." Lacy tugged again to no avail.

Sellars shook her head, her grip twisting on the steering wheel.

Lacy reached for the answer. "You were driving. That's it, isn't it?" She grabbed for the truth.

"Don't." Sellars finally looked away from the window and pinned a hard stare on Lacy. Her eyes glistened with the panel lights. "Just...don't."

"Don't what? Don't ask you to open up? The same way you asked me to? The same way you dug into my dark little secrets?" Lacy yanked at the seat belt a little harder. "What's wrong, Sellars? Do I need to get naked and fuck you on the hood of the car to get some answers? Or are you the only one allowed to play by that rule?"

Sellars's expression softened. "That's not…I didn't…" She clamped her lips and turned back to the window. "Get out."

"What happened to your girlfriend, Sellars?" Lacy asked, determined to break the barrier. "It's just you and me. No one else. Talk to me."

"Get out!" Sellars bellowed and punched her fist against the door panel.

Lacy stopped tugging at the seat belt at the sound. There was so much pain locked inside of Sellars. Why wouldn't she just say it? What the hell had she done?

"No! Dammit." Lacy gave a little tug on the buckle once again. "Talk to me. Fucking get it off your chest. Out in the open. Once and for all. Get the fuck out of your own head, Sellars!" She yanked at the seat belt, harder, desperate to be free of the confinement.

Long silence followed while Lacy tried in vain to get the lock to release. "In case you haven't noticed, I'm kind of locked in here."

Sellars reached out across the distance between them, squeezed the sides in on the seat belt, and the lock popped loose.

When Lacy turned to thank her, to take in a deep breath now that the claustrophobia had been squelched, she found Sellars staring at her. Her eyes were full of tears.

"I killed her."

CHAPTER FIFTEEN

Instinct made Lacy swallow while the punch of Sellars's words settled in. She resisted reaching for the door handle. Resisted looking away. Afraid the fear was crystal clear in her eyes.

Her voice had been so quiet, Lacy wasn't sure she'd heard the words right. Prayed she hadn't heard them right.

But the look of despair, the pain in those eyes, told Lacy she'd heard exactly what she thought she had heard.

"Keep going." Lacy fought the urge to reach out and take her hand while a little voice screamed to get her dumb ass out of the car. To run like the hounds of hell were on her heels. To never look back.

But those words, the softness in them, hadn't come from a murderer.

Sellars took in a breath and slowly let it out. "We were in high school. Sonny and Cher. Fred and Ethel. Lucy and Ricky. Bonny. Clyde. I was trouble. Liked disobeying. Determined my parents weren't going to force me into their little outline of how they expected my life to turn out. She loved me so much, she was willing to come along for the ride. Every ride."

She turned and looked out the window. "She was the only one who ever believed in me. She got me. All of me. She got all of me. My desire to race. My hatred for the medical college my mom had already pre-selected, no doubt from the minute I was born."

Lacy watched as Sellars released her grip on the steering wheel only to tighten it again.

She realized she was hanging on every word. Desperate for those answers, desperate to know Sellars's disturbing secret.

"We had a vow. I would make it all the way up, up those rungs of success despite my family, to the top, to NASCAR, and she would be there waiting for me at the finish line. She promised to be there. I promised to make it there."

Sellars hung her head. "And then she was gone."

Lacy waited with bated breath. She could almost see Sellars's mental struggle as her jaw clenched.

"A simple road race. Like all the rest. With her right by my side. A deer. Just a goddamn deer," Sellars spat. "It came out of nowhere. I swerved. I…swerved." Her voice lowered into a whisper. "I killed her."

Lacy lifted her hand to reach out to Sellars, then she thought better of it. Sellars was an open book right now. Touching her would bring her back to reality.

She could almost see the detailed images in her own mind as she absorbed the facts.

Sellars, young, high schooler, probably underage, probably drinking because that's what punk high schoolers did, maybe even a little weed, the road race, no doubt on some back road, the deer, swerving to miss it, a mistake an uneducated driver would make, and the girlfriend was killed.

Granddaddy had swooped in to save the day, for sure. It all made sense.

But what didn't make sense was why she hated him. How did that make him a monster? How did that make his money blood red? Wouldn't a person want their family to save the day? To make the merry-go-round stop?

Lacy wanted to ask, but she knew the sound of her voice would break the spell. Nor did she want to ruin the moment.

She wasn't sure, but she'd bet Billy's next checkered flag that Sellars didn't share this information with many people. Possibly none at all.

"I should have died that night." Sellars choked out her words. "It should have been me."

And there it was. The guilt. Guilt she'd taken along for the ride during every race. Every race, she'd taken those memories with her. Her guilt had been the passenger. Her copilot.

Lacy wished she had the right words, but there were none.

The cliché, "Everything's going to be okay. It wasn't your fault" paled in comparison to the guilt Sellars had already strapped around herself.

Those words wouldn't fix her.

But that finish line would. That was her goal, right? To cross that line. For the girlfriend. To keep good on a promise.

Yet Sellars had unsuccessfully sabotaged every step of her success. Somehow, she'd stumbled over every finish line of Formula One despite her own mental punishment.

And here she was, one step away from beginning a brand new career with NASCAR, her dreams dangling by a thread.

Why? She was good enough to get there. All by herself.

She probably could have been there long before now. Actually, with her skill, she should have been here long before now.

So, what was holding her back? Why did she keep getting in her own way?

"Bullshit." The word was out of Lacy's mouth before she could stop it.

Worse, she meant it. She was calling bullshit because that was a line of bullshit Sellars was feeding her.

Sellars turned a glare on her, eyes full of anger and pain and tears. "Are you serious?"

"Yes. It's all bullshit. You can't sabotage your career and get to that finish line at the same time. You're smart enough to know that. Yet you do. Everything you do is a roadblock to that finish line."

"Get the hell out of the car."

Lacy turned in the seat to face her. "You don't want to cross that finish line, do you? You don't want to win. That's why you veered off the path. Why you went for Formula One instead of going straight for your goal. Because as long as you don't win, as long as that checkered flag of NASCAR, your destination, never waves above your car, you can carry all that guilt around with you while blaming the world for your downfall."

Lacy knew she should stop. Sellars had just poured her heart out. Lacy should have some compassion. But how could she when the truth was staring her in the face?

She barreled on, determined to say every word on her mind. "While hating your grandfather because he did the only thing he could do. He used his money to make your dilemma go away because that's the only fucking thing he could do."

"Get out, Lacy."

Lacy narrowed her sights. "You are your own worst enemy, Sellars. So, shit or get off the pot. Either give that girl what you promised or stop wasting everyone's time."

Anger rippled through Lacy. She wasn't sure what she was so upset about. Sellars for still blaming everyone else for her own doings? Or herself for being entirely too honest when it came to the thoughts in her mind.

She, too, needed to get her own shit together. She needed to stop running from a demon that wasn't even chasing her. The fucker was in her own mind. Not real. Yet she continued to run.

No more. No fucking more.

Lacy searched for the door handle, realized there wasn't one, then climbed out of the car before Sellars could respond.

Guilt ate at her as she turned back to the window, taking in the pained and shocked expression on Sellars's face.

"You can't even say her name, can you?" Lacy said.

Sellars's jaw clenched.

"You've got her so locked up inside that mind of yours because you don't want to share her. You're holding a ghost like her life depends on it." Lacy put her hands on the frame and leaned down farther. "Her life doesn't depend on it. Yours does!"

Sellars squeezed the steering wheel and turned to look out the windshield.

"Look at me, dammit!" Lacy yelled.

Sellars turned steely eyes on her.

"Say it, Sellars. Say her name."

The tears welled in Sellars's eyes, but she didn't turn away.

"Say it," Lacy whispered.

"Sarah." Sellars turned away. "Her name was Sarah."

Lacy stood. More words were on the tip of her tongue. Harsh words. Honest words. But she couldn't say them. Not now.

Sellars had had enough.

Lacy turned around and jogged to the sidewalk where Jared met her. With a grunt, she kicked out of the suit.

What she wouldn't give to run back to Sellars, to hug her, to tell her everything was going to be okay. She needed to tell her that it really wasn't her fault, but she couldn't. Fact was, only Sellars knew if everything was going to be all right. The power was in her hands. Her hands and hers alone.

That night might not have been her fault, but every step of the way since that horrible moment had been in her control, and Lacy lacked the proper medical degree to get inside her head and repair the engine.

Chapter Sixteen

Sellars opened her eyes to bright sunshine filtering through the edge of the blanket hung over the window. She hissed as her head thundered in objection.

With a groan, she rolled onto her side, turning her back into the light, and attempted to crack her eyes open again.

She had no idea what time it was. Hell, after all the beer she'd consumed last night, she prayed she knew what day it was, and that she hadn't been comatose for more than twenty-four hours.

When the light didn't make her head scream in pain again, she reached for the phone on the floor and found the evidence that she'd put a serious hurting on a case of beer.

She'd surely pay a high price for that today.

But who the hell did Lacy think she was talking to her like that? Making her feel guilty for feeling guilty. Who does that after someone pours their heart out?

Not anyone with a heart, that's for sure.

Lacy. Pfft. Who needed Lacy? Or her photographer skills?

No. She didn't need Lacy's help. Not anyone's help, as a matter of fact. But especially not Lacy's.

And her grandfather could go straight to hell. If she had to give up this dream, so be it, but she wanted nothing more to do with him or his fat bank account or the way he could so easily brush her broken heart away with dollar bills.

She would find a way to do this on her own. Somehow.

With her head pounding, she finally sat on the edge of the bed and looked around. No furniture. No pictures. Not even curtains.

There was no girlfriend to share life with. Probably never would be. And somehow, she was okay with that, no matter what that stupid little voice tried to whisper.

She was okay with being alone. Her way. Everything her way.

But something in the back of her mind said she was being ridiculous. She'd gotten a taste of someone she almost hated. The sweet taste that still hummed in the back of her mind. On the back of her tongue.

Sellars shoved off the bed and grabbed her clothing from the carpet. She donned each piece and went to the kitchen, hoping there was more beer left in the fridge.

Thankfully, there was. She snapped off the top and turned up the bottle, letting the cool malt slide down her throat, wishing it could take away her thoughts just as easily.

The thoughts of Lacy being so cold last night. The sight of her racing back up those stairs and disappearing into the building.

It was the last she'd seen of her. Gone. She'd been gone when Sellars finally managed to pull herself together and climb out, no doubt by the means of an Uber.

Sellars had never met anyone so heartless, and the sound of her words vibrating against her mind pissed her off all over again.

She downed the rest of the bottle, chucked it in the sink, and slipped out into the sun that was just beginning to set behind the trees.

Damn. She'd slept the whole day away in her drunken state.

That was okay. She was going to do the very same thing tonight. Maybe this time, she'd get lucky enough to find a woman to squirm beneath her. Yes. That's exactly what she needed. A woman to hiss and scream, proving to Sellars that she was alive.

Yes. She needed that feeling. That emotion.

With determination, she started walking until she found a sports bar. Right where she wanted to be.

As soon as she sidled up to the bar, a brunette at the opposite end flashed her a wicked smile and followed it up with a sultry wink.

For sure, this night was going to end well.

❖

Lacy paced the conference room, waiting for Mr. Reynolds to grace her with his presence. She wasn't sure why she was so restless. She knew exactly what she wanted to say to this man. The exact order in which she wanted to say the words. She would say them with no hesitation and without compassion because that was the only way she knew how.

Running into Sellars. That was the reason she couldn't stand still. She was afraid of seeing her, of seeing the hurt in her eyes again, and not acting on it again.

Did she regret the things she'd said last night? Of course not. She didn't do regrets. What she did hate was the fact that she'd had to say anything at all. That, clearly, no one had said those words before now. That she wasn't able to just hug her, to give her a shoulder to cry on.

That's what was wrong with Sellars. No one had ever crossed her. They'd just let her go on her merry way, demolishing everything in her path, destroying her future.

Not Lacy. There were no other words she could have said last night.

However, she'd stayed up into the wee hours of the morning waiting to hear the rumble of Sellars's car in the driveway. Hour after hour, she'd waited for that sound. It hadn't come. Either Sellars had gone to her apartment to sleep on a bed in a place that didn't even have mini blinds, or she'd found a piece of ass. The latter was likely the outcome. That's how Sellars rolled. She just kept going on that dead-end path, no matter what.

The last option ate at her more than anything. That green-eyed monster that she had mastered years ago. She didn't do jealousy. It wasn't becoming. Not to mention one should never have to be jealous. Jealousy equaled non-trust. And if she couldn't trust someone, she damn sure didn't want them.

But no matter how much she reminded herself of that fact, her gut continued to knot every time she thought of Sellars fucking someone else. The image of her down on her knees, between someone else's thighs, was more than Lacy could handle.

Mr. Reynolds strolled into the room like Lacy was an afterthought, just another meeting he was forced to endure from his calendar, dragging Lacy from her too-clear images.

"Lacy, so great to see you." He gave her arm a squeeze. "I must say, I'm pleased that you've kept Sellars out of trouble and to the schedule. Very pleased, indeed."

"Thank you, but I've actually come to tell you in person that you'll have to find someone else to babysit."

He tilted his head like he hadn't understood. Probably because he wasn't used to having someone turn him down. Maybe that trait ran in the family. "What about our agreement? For your cause."

"Sellars doesn't need a makeover, or a fundraising event, or photo ops cuddling cute little puppies." Lacy squared her sights on him. "She needs you, Mr. Reynolds. Not the you that can pay away her troubles. Not the you that is large and in charge with his name all over this city. She needs *you*, the granddaddy."

He furrowed his brow. "She's always had me."

"No, she's had what you could buy her. She had all the ways your money could buy her out of mischief." Lacy turned her gaze out the window.

"Isn't that what family is supposed to do?"

Lacy turned back to him. His expression was genuine. He had no clue what he was doing wrong. "Give her a fucking hug, Mr. Reynolds. That's what family does. They have each other's back but won't hesitate to kick ass if one misbehaves." She lowered her voice. "I know you love her. Now show it without your checkbook."

He gave her a tight nod. "I do. I love her very much. She makes it hard to show it sometimes."

"Then just hug her." Lacy took a step toward him. "That's all she needs. And then you can scold her like any grandfather would do. Tell her you're done with her shit and if she doesn't shape up, you'll ship her out and replace her with someone who deserves the spot. And mean it when you say it."

A smile transformed on his face. "She's special, that one. Always has been. Never one to follow the rules. Especially her parents. She broke my daughter's heart when she left college. Broke it again when she announced she was going to be a race car driver."

Lacy considered his words and found sadness in them. She had a sneaky suspicion that Sellars didn't know she'd broken her family's hearts. That she'd specifically hurt her mother. She also believed that Sellars's mother had never have offered those words either. They were that kind of family. Where everyone kept their feelings to themselves.

And yes, Sellars was special. She had a special gift that would take her far on the track. Hopefully, she'd find out how special she could be in this life as well, and the worlds would combine and make her one hell of a race car challenger.

"It's almost too late to reel her back in, Mr. Reynolds. Don't waste time."

"Is there anything I can do to change your mind?"

"No, sir. I can't help her. But you can."

"I'm disappointed, but I understand. Can I at least pay you for the time you've invested in Sellars?" He reached inside the front pocket of his jacket.

"Please. Keep your money. To be honest, I don't want it tarnishing my life the way Sellars believes it's tainted hers."

He turned to look up at her with a startled expression. "She told you?"

The shocked look proved that Lacy was right. Sellars didn't share that dirty little secret with others.

"Not everything, but it doesn't take a genius to put the pieces together. I don't know the whole story. I don't need to know all of it. But what I do know, she doesn't need your money anymore. She needs you."

He gave a timid smile and nodded. "Thank you, Lacy. For everything. But especially your thoughtful words."

Lacy turned for the elevator.

"Wait. What about the photographer's job? I truly meant that, Lacy. That offer stood apart from Sellars. It's yours for the taking."

Lacy didn't need to think about the answer. She didn't need to think about anything. Her mind had been made up since she walked away from that racetrack.

She pushed the down button and the doors slid open. With a quick breath, she stepped inside and turned to face him. "Give the job to Leonard Curshaw from the *Wicked Truth*. He's a journalist and a photographer and could use a career change. He's a stone cold heartless cunt who gets off on sick chaos. It has nothing to do with me being a woman and him being a man. It has to do with me having a heart and him being a raunchy prick. The job would be perfect for him."

The doors slid shut and Lacy smiled. Freedom. Change. She could see it. And she was going to reach it. That dream photography job, back on the track where she used to feel the most freedom, wasn't so dreamy after all. The dream job was nothing more than a nightmare.

She just wanted out of this building, out of this city, on a plane and headed home so she could start making those life-altering changes. To a home that was truly never home at all. It was simply a place she landed to bury her head in the sand.

No more. No more hiding. No more running.

She had people, helpless people, depending on her to get her shit together. To put the pieces together for their benefit.

That, she damn well would do.

It was time to orchestrate her next plan of action. One that she couldn't back down from. One she would shove through all the red tape to accomplish.

She could do it if she'd stop being so prideful. If she asked for help, let someone assist, she could do this. Of that, she was certain.

With a little financial backing, she could do wonders. *Our World Through Their Eyes* was going to breathe life one way or the other.

The time had come to make a difference in their lives. In her own.

In other words, she needed to practice what she preached. She needed to shit or get off the pot.

❖

Sellars tossed the shot of tequila back and rose from the stool to go introduce herself to the beauty still eye-fucking her from the end of the counter. She was actually more surprised that it had taken her much longer than it normally did to say hello and then head for a bedroom. Maybe it was the lingering hangover slowing her down.

She took several steps across the floor when she noticed a man feeding pigeons from a bench on the sidewalk.

She recognized him. Ralph? Yes. The homeless man Lacy seemed to adore. The man Lacy had fed at McDonald's. The man Sellars had barely spoken to while he tucked a cheeseburger into his pocket like a squirrel hiding nuts, while Lacy conversed with him like she was catching up on life.

The need to get to the beauty near her, the one only feet away from her, was strong, but not nearly as strong as the need to go talk to the man outside was.

She tossed a twenty on the counter and stepped outside, hoping the possibility would still be available later. She truly needed sex.

Ralph looked up from his bent position, scanning her. Not out of curiosity. But out of fear.

He expected her to run him off. The thought made her sad. He was doing nothing wrong, yet she had no doubt he'd been run off of benches or corners or alleys many times for doing nothing more than feeding the hungry birds.

"Aren't you Lacy's friend? Ralph?" Sellars circled around to the front of the bench, hoping she didn't startle him further.

His face lit up at the mention of Lacy's name.

Sellars understood why. She lit up with the thoughts of her, too. Well, not in the last twenty-four hours. Shit. Even that was a lie. She hadn't been able to stop thinking about her. Even when she was mad as hell at her harsh words, she'd wanted her.

Was Lacy the reason she hadn't been able to push herself off that stool sooner? Why she hadn't already left with the woman on her arm? Of course not. Being so angry was the reason. This hangover looming over her head was the answer.

But Lacy was special. No one was beneath her. Not even a homeless man.

"Yes." He smiled, but Sellars could still feel his worry.

So she sat down beside him so she wasn't hovering above him and noticed the wedding band on his finger. "Are you married?"

He looked away and tossed more pieces of bread onto the sidewalk. "I was. I lost her. To cancer."

"I'm sorry."

He tossed another chunk of bread and didn't offer a response.

Sellars didn't want the conversation to end when it really hadn't had a chance to begin. Lacy had learned something through these people. Possibly this man. She wanted to know what that was. And how. "So how did you meet Lacy?"

A smile curved his lips again. "She was serving food at the soup kitchen." He tossed out another piece of bread. "Lacy wasn't like the others. Oh sure, they were polite while they fed us, but there was pity in their eyes."

Sellars smiled. Lacy didn't pity people. Not because she didn't care. But because she wasn't above them. Pity came from being better than someone. From having more than them. From knowing it.

No doubt, Lacy would treat a janitor with the exact same respect she would treat a CEO.

God, she loved that about her.

"Lacy not only served us food, she grabbed herself a plate and sat right down with us, like she was part of the family, like she was one of us. She even took off her shoes." He chuckled, turned the bag up, and emptied the crumbs for the birds. "And she hugged every one of us like she loved us."

Without knowing why, Sellars knew that hug was important. Not just to Ralph, but to all of them.

"That sounds like Lacy," Sellars said. "What little I've learned about her."

There was so much more she'd wanted to learn. So many more times she'd wanted to shut that mouth, to silence that tongue. Damn, how she wanted to silence that tongue. Again. And again.

He nodded and looked out over the city. "You can ask, if you want. It's okay."

"Ask you about what?" Sellars leaned up, suddenly aware that her entire attention was on this man while a free piece of ass was waiting for her inside the bar. A piece of ass she truly hadn't been interested in.

When had that happened? Why had it happened, was the better question.

And she was perfectly okay with whatever the answer was. Being with Ralph here, with the answer to the deepest question of all, was all that mattered. All she cared about.

"How I got here. On these streets." He turned clear eyes on her. "Everyone wants to know."

Sellars hadn't known she wanted to know until now. "So how did you get here, Ralph?"

He settled back against the seat and gave her a curious stare. "You remind me of myself, you know? In the bars. Pretty women in your line of sights. Never alone unless you want to be. I was like that. A long time ago. I liked the women. I liked being the center of someone's attention. I think it made me feel wanted, important, alive. Does that sound like you?"

Yes, as a matter of fact, it sounded exactly like her. But not because she needed to feel those emotions, but because she couldn't feel them. Hadn't felt them in so damn long.

Until Lacy, that is. Those cries of passion, that sharp tongue slicing her down to size, correcting her and scolding her, made her realize how much she needed that attention.

"Yes."

"I come to sit outside this bar to remind myself why I deserve to live on the streets."

Sellars said nothing while he nodded toward the intersection.

"Right there, in that walkway, is where my life ended."

"What happened?"

He was silent for many long seconds, so long that Sellars was worried he was going to leave her hanging without the ending.

"My wife was dying. Cancer was going to take the love of my life away from me. The person who got me. The person who made me stop seeing how pretty the women were."

He drew in a breath. "She was always by my side. She loved me so much I didn't think I could ever deserve that love. And there she was, dying. Leaving me. So I would come here to drink away my pathetic sorrow. To wallow in my tears. As if she wasn't the one lying there in unbearable pain. As if she wasn't terrified of dying." He shifted on the seat but kept his gaze trained on the walkway light. "So I came here. Drank until I couldn't walk, let alone drive. Met a pretty little thing that night. Flirty. Damn, she was flirty. And sexy couldn't begin to describe her. So I fell for it. She was alive. My wife was dying."

He glanced down at the pigeons who had come to the conclusion that he was out of food and wandered closer to the building.

When he finally looked up, his sights went directly to the intersection. "So we stumbled out here, on this sidewalk, and finally managed to get in the car parked by the crosswalk. I had a cool car. A tar black Firebird with a gold eagle across the hood. A guy car. Chick magnet, if you know what I mean."

Sellars knew what he meant. She drove a car with the same personality. Hearing him say those words made her feel a little guilty, selfish, self-centered, to own it.

"She was my cruising through the city car. Pick up girls car. Then I met Abby. She loved it. She always made me take the top down so she could inhale the air. Couldn't bring myself to part with it even after we got married."

Sellars detected the catch in his voice but didn't want to pat his back or say a word, afraid he would change his mind about the heart to heart.

"Right here, in front of this bar, that night, we made out in the back seat. I had sex with a woman and I didn't even know her name. All because I was lonely. Because I was a coward. Because God was taking away the only thing I loved in this life. And when it was over, when we awkwardly put our clothes back on, I hated myself. I hated her. The guilt was like a soul eater. Sucking the life out of me. And I hated myself so bad I couldn't get away from her fast enough."

Sellars resisted the urge to reach out for his arm. Lacy would have. She would have curled up in this man's lap and encouraged him to get it all out. But Sellars couldn't. She didn't know how to.

"As soon as she got out of the car, I floored it." He pointed to the light that had a blue hand blinking and the timer displaying thirteen seconds left to cross. "And then, he was there. Running across the road. He came out of nowhere."

Sellars could see the images clearly. She could see them because she'd lived them once before. Out of nowhere. The very thing to change your life forever had come out of nowhere. And then the life you loved so much, simply died.

"He died right there in the middle of that intersection. I went to jail. All night. Drunk. Puking. Hating myself. When the judge finally released me, after witnesses came to give their police reports, I broke every speed limit to get back to her. To beg her forgiveness. To never leave her side again until God decided it was time." His words dropped off and a sob left his lips. "When I walked into my own house the next morning, my wife was dead."

Another sob escaped, and Sellars finally reached out and squeezed his shoulder.

"She died all alone because of me. No one to kiss her cheek. No one to hold her hand. No one. No one. Because I was—because I am—a worthless coward who deserves to live on these streets until I take my last breath. I deserve to die out here all alone. Just like she did."

Sellars gave another quick squeeze, feeling a little out of her element while feeling directly in it. "I'm so sorry."

"I appreciate that. But I don't deserve anyone's pity. I did this to myself."

Suddenly, Sellars was looking inside herself. She, too, was carrying a load very similar. Guilt. Regret. Feeling that she deserved all the bad things around her because those bad things had happened to someone else instead.

Hearing him say those words out loud, how much she disagreed with them, she understood exactly what Lacy was trying to tell her.

Bullshit. Everything she'd been doing was bullshit. She'd been lying to herself all along.

Lacy was right. Sellars was in her own way. Sabotaging her own success. Why? Because she didn't think she deserved it? Because she didn't want to lose the memories of Sarah?

How could she? Sarah would always be in her thoughts. She would always be a part of Sellars. Every race, every win, every award, she would share some of the glory with Sarah. Sarah and only Sarah had pushed Sellars to be exactly what she wanted to be.

And she'd done that. She'd left her family behind to go live her dream. She'd taken a chance that they would never speak to her again to go after her own life.

Yet she'd put up her own roadblocks to keep from reaching the goal.

Damn. Lacy might not have delivered her message in the most delicate way, but she'd delivered it nonetheless. Sellars got it now. She heard her.

"Yes, you did. You did a stupid, irresponsible thing." Sellars said the words before she could change her mind. "But do you deserve a life sentence because of it?"

Ralph turned to look at her, and a smile creased the corner of his mouth. "You sound like Lacy."

His words were a bigger compliment than he would ever know. "Tell me, if your wife didn't have cancer, and you'd cheated on her, would she have forgiven you? Honestly."

He looked away and shrugged. "I think so. Yes."

"Then she forgave you a long time ago, and this punishment you cast on yourself, is only hurting her. If she's as wonderful as you described her, she wouldn't want to see you live with so much guilt."

The urge to rush back to her apartment, grab her car, drive like a maniac, breaking every speed limit, slow drivers be damned, to get to Lacy, overwhelmed Sellars.

Lacy was right. She'd been right all along.

Sellars was her own worst enemy. She'd done this to herself, not caring who she hurt, to keep Sarah alive.

Keeping her alive was impossible. A horrible accident, one that wasn't her fault, had taken her life. It was time to set Sarah free. To set herself free.

"Wow. No one besides Lacy has ever been so direct." Ralph chuckled.

"Sorry. I guess she's rubbing off on me."

"That's never a bad thing." Ralph patted her leg. "Lacy is one of a kind."

"Ralph, it's been great talking to you. Thank you for sharing your story." Sellars pushed off the bench and extended her hand. "It's reminded me that I owe someone an apology for being a jerk."

Ralph took her hand and gave it a firm squeeze. "Good luck to you. I hope Lacy forgives you."

Sellars cocked her head. "I didn't say Lacy."

He winked. "You didn't have to. Go. Go make your amends."

Thirty minutes later, Sellars all but slid into Billy's driveway.

Her heart was hammering, but she was mentally lighter. No one had ever spoken to her the way Lacy had. No one had ever called her bluff.

It was hot. If only she hadn't been so mad. So hurt. So open and vulnerable.

And stunned. She'd been stunned that someone had shoved back so hard. No one had ever been so blunt.

She bolted out of the car and jogged down the sidewalk, determined to get to Lacy, to kiss her, to ask her forgiveness, and then to thank her. To thank her for being so right. She'd been keeping Sarah's memory alive through mischief and bad behavior, by veering off the designated path, terrified she would truly be gone when she finally crossed that finish line.

But right now, with the sun sinking behind the trees, with this weightless feeling engulfing her, with her heart full, she knew Sarah was already gone. She had Lacy to thank for that.

From this day forward, she was going to live this damn life like a great one awaited her. She was going to cross that line. She was going to conquer every race. And she was going to do it for herself.

She practically ran into the locked door and had to stall long enough to fumble for the keys.

Finally, she found the right one and threw the door open. The sound of silence surrounded her.

Total silence. No Lacy cussing at the kitchen counter. No Billy teasing Lacy to get a rise out of her. No Gabby tapping that swear jar every time Lacy opened her mouth. No Darlene smiling at all of them with love and devotion.

She immediately missed the chatter. It was too quiet. She hated the quiet. Missed Lacy's sharp tongue that was sure to put Gabby through college. She loved that about her even more. How much she loved this family.

She wanted that. A family of her own. Exactly like this one. She wanted to hear Lacy cuss while she was cooking. Wanted to hear her kids' footsteps racing down a flight of steps. She wanted to throw a football or paint fingernails. She wanted a freaking swear jar on her own kitchen counter.

Did Lacy want those things as well? Did she want a family of her own? One to blend with this one?

Why was it so damn quiet? Where the hell was everyone? Grandma's. They'd decided to stay longer at Grandma's.

That meant that Lacy was here. Alone. In the basement. A place she'd been banished to because Sellars was too stubborn to give up a room that had Lacy written all over it, starting with a drawer full of thongs and other delicate feminine underwear.

She bolted across the room with the knowledge that they were alone and threw open the man cave door. Unable to control her need to get to Lacy, she took the steps two at a time until she landed on the basement carpet.

If only she'd stopped Lacy last night. If only she hadn't been so angry that Lacy had been so cruel. She should have run after her like she'd wanted to. She should have stopped her, kissed her, exactly like she'd wanted. Instead, she'd watched her walk away with her own ego bruised from the truth.

Right here, right now, she was finally free. No more guilt. No more trouble. No more resisting her own success.

Except the room was empty.

Sellars paced to the bathroom, praying Lacy was in there, naked.

The door was ajar. No Lacy.

She pushed open the bedroom door. No Lacy.

When she looked back toward the open living area, she spotted a piece of paper propped up on the coffee table.

She slowly walked to it, terrified it was meant for her, that it would say good-bye forever.

With her breath caught in her throat, she reached down and picked up the note.

Sellars,

I do have a price tag. It's called pride. You should find your own. Good luck at your finish line.

Lacy.

CHAPTER SEVENTEEN

Lacy curled up cross-legged on the ottoman, took another sip of wine, and fanned through the last of the photos Patrick had picked up from the homeless shelter and post office on his way to her apartment.

This was it. The last of the disposable cameras before show time.

Her heart quickened with the thought. They were so close to either making this dream come true or bombing altogether.

"This is amazing." Patrick tapped her arm with a picture from his perch on the floor. "These guys are getting more creative."

Lacy took the photo and held it out then took another sip of wine. She did that a lot. Sipped wine.

It mellowed her. Why she wasn't mellow without it was a mystery. She'd already handed over all of her contracts to another photographer. Most, she'd gleefully given away. It didn't take a professional photographer to read some people. They were trouble in waiting. Another bridezilla she had no desire to work for.

She'd never been happier to say that she was jobless. No career in the future. And no desire to figure out what she wanted to be when she grew up. That she currently had nothing more than her savings account to pay her bills, and as of now, was possibly a year away from panic mode, and she was perfectly okay with that.

Right now, she just wanted to concentrate on getting this project off the ground. These men and women needed her help. And they were basically doing the hard work themselves.

For example, the picture she was holding in her hand. An abandoned building dominated the photo. Something that resembled an old smokehouse. Maybe a shed. The roof was decayed and one section caved in, stripping the true nature of what the structure once was. Around the perimeter, vintage signs were scattered on the ground. She could make out Coca-Cola, Ford, and another that had the barbershop twirl post. Most were rusted and unreadable, giving an antique quality to the surrounding.

There was no color to any of the photos, as she and Patrick had both declared that black and white gave more of a punch. And they were right. Each and every photo held a past while living in the present. It was their present. Their current lives.

Black and white was the only color of choice for the people who fought to survive every day. Who knew more about these streets, had witnessed even more than any person could imagine. Like the hundreds before them. Even more before them. A pattern Lacy and Patrick hoped to destroy with this project.

"This is insane," Lacy said before she placed it in the pile that would be shipped to the Art Lounge in Pittsburgh.

After returning from her vacation, early, thanks to Sellars, she'd hit the ground running. She'd sent emails, left voice mails, and shot texts to every art studio she could find in Pittsburgh. In the city as well as surrounding perimeter. Praying someone in the city—in her city—in the place that had wrapped her in love for years, would reach out. She couldn't think of a more fitting area to debut these amazing photographs, starring the men and women who lived this life every day. Who begged for a little help.

Once those photos went on display, she knew no one would pass those precious souls by again. No one would ever look at them the same again.

Days had gone by after the last email went out, giving Lacy time to feel down on her luck, to believe that no one was going to help, and just when she was beginning to think this pet project was never going to lift off the ground, Shelley, who owned a studio in the heart of the city, where the hometown crowd walked daily, where tourists visited weekly, was extremely interested in their project, and offered Lacy and Patrick the entire space, free of charge. To add to the excitement, she'd offered to provide all necessary equipment. She even called several days later with a caterer who would donate all food and drinks as long as they could display their own business name for advertisement.

The single response had been the good luck they'd needed. The rest had fallen into place like rocks tumbling down a mountainside. A local beer distributor would provide the alcohol. Another would donate wine and glasses. The list continued growing with so many people who were willing to lend a helping hand in some form or another.

It was happening. Their dream, a dream that had started out as a "what-if" conversation, was alive.

Lacy hadn't stopped running since. Wouldn't stop. She couldn't. When she stopped, images flooded.

So she kept moving. Kept her mind occupied. And kept sipping that damn wine.

Soon, every town, city, and state would hop on board. She had faith it would happen.

And they would. She was confident of that. And it would all begin in Pittsburgh, where it had all started for her, where she'd met Ralph, heard his story, and felt the compassion to do more.

Patrick sighed. "And this one. Would you just look at that waterfall?"

Lacy took the photo. A lazy river winding through a forest dominated the picture with the waterfall in the distance.

She immediately thought of Sellars. Dammit. She'd kissed her the first time while standing over water. While a fountain hissed nearby.

Lacy thought of her often. It was hard not to think about her when the news continued to flash her face, her car, her achievements, all over the television. She couldn't get away from her no matter how hard she tried. The magazines at the checkout. The radio. She was everywhere.

And she'd finally crossed that finish line. Not as the winner, but as a finisher, and that was just as amazing.

Lacy wondered if she'd left her memories on the track. If she'd conquered her demons with the wave of the flag.

To be honest, Lacy was downright proud of her. She'd proven Lacy wrong. Proved everyone wrong. For sure, Lacy never dreamed she'd make it to the track, let alone a finish line. Not out of handcuffs, anyway.

But she had, and she still looked just as sexy now as she had two months ago wearing that race suit, with Lacy digging the imaginary knife even deeper with her words, calling her story bullshit.

Yes. She'd done that. She'd mentally punched someone who had finally cracked open the shell and allowed Lacy to see the dirty little secrets. She'd shown Lacy what made her tick. What had motivated her.

Damn. She'd been such a jerk. Hopefully, some of her words, any of her words, had been the shove she needed to make it to the finish line. She could only hope.

Lacy had been just as proud of herself. She'd actually watched a race without feeling the need to throw up. Without sweat running down her neck. Without holding her breath.

That old saying was right. When it was your time, the grim reaper would find you no matter where you were.

Nah. She still called bullshit on that one. Truth was, if you kept yourself out of harm's way, the likelihood was slim.

Patrick would laugh at her conclusion, as he often did when she mentioned Billy on the track, how terrified she was, how he was going to die in a curve. "If the grim reaper doesn't get Billy on the racetrack, he'll get him in a recliner, watching the weather report with little Gabby. He's gonna get you. Any of us. All of us. Period and end of discussion. Down off soapbox." He would always end with that little finger snap of conclusion, ending the discussion.

Maybe he was right.

Either way, Sellars had shaken herself out of trouble and she was going to climb higher in those rankings. She was going to be the storm they never saw coming. And soon, she was going to watch Brett in her rearview mirror.

He deserved nothing less after unloading such a bombshell. Only insecure nimrods went below the belt.

Then again, Sellars had jacked his wife up against a brick wall in an alley, with cell phones to capture the blissful moment.

Patrick tapped another picture against her leg, and Lacy blinked out of her oncoming heated thoughts, as well as the green-eyed monster that always followed closely behind when another woman was in those thoughts with Sellars. Without someone else intruding, those thoughts of Sellars always led to heat. Usually led to her masturbating. Too often.

Honestly, if she was forced to be honest with herself, she missed Sellars. Missed what, she wasn't sure. Sellars had been a broken mess. Lacy didn't do broken messes. If anything, she created them. Not deliberately. But with brutal honesty.

The same kind of honesty she'd shot at Sellars.

She regretted that the most. That she hadn't hugged Sellars when she possibly needed a hug after her uncovering. That she hadn't told Sellars that Sarah's death wasn't her fault. She'd possibly never heard those words before. Not from her grandfather. Not from her parents. Maybe not at all. Ever. That sucked the most.

But it was too late now. And she'd meant every word. Every cutting syllable, she'd meant. Every. Single. One.

Maybe she could have delivered them differently. With less of a punch.

She almost snorted as she took the photo from Patrick.

Since when had she ever regretted telling people off? Since when did she wonder if her words had left a scar? Since when?

Since she'd fallen for someone who couldn't even love herself. That's when.

Yes. Dammit. She'd done that. Fallen for someone who carried her demons around like a prized possession. Who had created chaos and destruction just to keep her guilt alive. Because she thought she deserved nothing less than horrible things.

"You like it?" Patrick looked up.

Lacy ripped the thoughts out of her head and focused on the picture. "Yes. I love all of them. We're going to need more frames."

Patrick looked back down at the thinning stack in his lap. "Done. I snuck a peek of them at the photo lab before I left and knew you'd love them just as much as I did. Got a whole case of frames in the car."

Lacy smiled. "This show is going to be spectacular."

"Explosive," Patrick added. "We're going to rock their worlds."

She prayed.

They only had one shot to do this right. Even with the studio handout and all the other freebies offered out of the hearts of many, there was so much more involved. So much more to take care of. So much more to worry about.

The radio station, the very one where Lacy had bared it all to save Sellars from a meltdown, was announcing the event several times a day. They owed her one as far as she was concerned.

She'd given the DJ a freebie flash, after all.

The newspaper was running articles thanks to Billy and his connections.

Everything was falling into place. Her dream was coming true. She was going to do something huge for Ralph and everyone just like him. For Pittsburgh, hopefully reaching farther, to more states, possibly global if the fates were with them.

So why did her heart catch every time she thought about their opening night?

Because she might run into Sellars. That's why.

She wasn't afraid of failing. She wasn't worried that people might think the project was a joke. She couldn't care less if people thought they had wasted their time. Nor did she give a shit if no one showed.

What choked her with fear was looking into Sellars's eyes once again. Those green eyes. The ones that sucked her in like a magical vortex.

She could do anything, but she wasn't sure she could do that.

Or inhale the scent of her. That unique scent.

Not to mention, what would she say?

"Hi, sexy. How have you been? Shake any demons lately?"

No. Of course not.

But simply saying hello, after so much unforgettable sex, after the images that had heated her thoughts daily, endlessly since she'd boarded that flight back home, seemed hilarious.

What were people supposed to say to someone they'd fucked, who was now part of your family? Sellars was part of Billy's family. Which made her part of Lacy's world.

How could she possibly act normal knowing that Billy had all but adopted her, that she would eventually be at Thanksgiving dinner, trading and stealing gifts over Christmas games, no doubt with a hot chick on her arm?

How could she possibly act normal when she knew she would have violent acts of death dancing in her mind while Sellars smooched her new fuck toy?

She didn't know how. But she damn well better figure it out fast.

Gabby thought Sellars was cool. She'd made a pal. Which meant Sellars wasn't going anywhere any time soon.

Lacy was trying to prepare herself for that upcoming encounter. It surely would happen. Anyone who was anyone would have heard about the event. Sellars would have heard Lacy's name dropped. She would know Lacy was coming.

And if by chance she had her head in the sand, or up some bitch's skirt, Billy would surely have made the announcement.

He'd already put the pieces together. Already concluded that Lacy had left without saying good-bye because, once again, she'd been running. And that more than babysitting had occurred.

She hated that about him. That he could read her without her opening her mouth. Actually, it was all the things she hadn't said that gave her away. Like, when he asked if she'd slept with Sellars and she'd changed the subject.

Yeah. That was smooth.

Bottom line was, Sellars would be there. Out of respect to the cause, to Billy, she would show up.

Dammit. She would.

Patrick tossed the last of the pictures onto the ottoman in front of her and pushed off the floor. "I love them all. It's impossible to choose just a few from that stack." He pushed his feet into a pair of flip-flops. "I'm going to buy more frames."

Lacy chuckled. "Just get them back over here before six and we can load them up with the shipment. Shipping company will be here not long after that."

He looked down at her with a smile. "We did it, chick. You. Then you and me. We did the damn thing."

Lacy set the wine glass on the coffee table, pushed the pictures out of her lap, and stood on the ottoman, her arms wide. "You're the best partner I could ever have. Hug me, dammit!"

He stepped into her embrace and squeezed her, pressing his cheek into her stomach. "I'm the happiest, saddest man in the world right now."

Lacy combed her fingers through his hair. She loved this man. He and his husband were the bestest friends a girl could ever have. They were her rock. If not for them, meeting them at a soup kitchen because she adored helping the local homeless, she wasn't so sure she would have found a comforting place in this bustling LA life.

"Don't be sad." Lacy squeezed him tighter.

"You're leaving me. For good." He faked a sniff. "Whatever will I do while Garrett is working all those long hours?"

"If luck is with us, in forty-eight hours, you're going to be running an office and getting our guys off the streets. You won't have time to miss me."

"That's bullshit and you know it." He finally loosened his grip and looked up at her. "I love your crazy, foul-mouthed self. I'll miss you so, so, so bad."

Lacy gave him a wink. "Ditto, kiddo." She stepped down off the chair. "Now, let's get this shit boxed and taped and ready for transport. Let the ending of hell begin."

Chapter Eighteen

Sellars maneuvered through the crowd gathered along the sidewalk outside the art studio. She stopped just shy of the door and glanced through the glass windows.

She could see the place was packed from wall to wall. People standing, some chatting and laughing, some moving slowly about the room.

She was nervous. Nervous to see Lacy again. Anxious, actually, to see her again.

No. She was desperate to see that face again. Desperate to look down into those tranquil, honest eyes. Desperate to kiss those lips. To silence that foul tongue.

Once again, she scanned the perimeter through the glass. Lacy was nowhere to be seen, but Sellars knew she was inside that building somewhere, and her stomach knotted.

She'd thought about this moment. What she would say. What Lacy would say. Would Lacy be cordial? Or would she tell Sellars to go to hell with her demons in tow?

Would she stop Sellars if, when, she tried to kiss her? Because she'd thought of nothing else for months now.

She'd wanted to reach out. To call her. To tell her that she missed her.

Fact was, she had a demon to slay first.

She'd done that. Destroyed her demon. And she'd done it by crossing that finish line, not finding Sarah there, not finding anyone there, as a matter of fact. But the most important person had been there.

Herself.

The burden of guilt had been lifted. The load had been left on the track. It was time for her to move forward in life. In her career. Time to shed the past and step into her future. The very future that she'd dreamed about before her foot could even reach a pedal. The very one her parents had tried to steal from her a long time ago.

She was living her dream. All along, she'd been living it. Only she'd been driving through it with sadness filling her heart. With guilt eating her soul.

She deserved to be here. And she deserved to be here guilt free.

Sarah would have been so proud. She'd always been so proud of Sellars.

Sellars scanned the crowd again just inside the glass but didn't spot Lacy.

A nervous chill snaked through her as she stepped around a couple who were admiring the photographs hanging in organized disarray inside the window, and she pushed open the double glass doors.

Warm air surrounded her as she took in a deep breath.

She needed to see Lacy's face. She needed to see that she was okay. A fact she already knew since she was constantly grilling Billy about her well-being. Terrified one day he would announce that there was a girlfriend in the picture. She wasn't sure her heart could take that kind of news.

Not after realizing after so many years, she'd fallen in love with someone. With someone who couldn't stand her.

Someone who made her stop seeing how gorgeous all the other women were.

She smiled as she thought of Ralph. He'd played a pivotal role in her life in the past few months. Keeping her on track. Keeping her spirits up.

Someone deliberately bumped into her.

Sellars turned to find Gabby by her side, that cute smile beaming up at her.

No wonder Lacy was in love with this kid. She was remarkable and fun and honest to a fault. Just like Lacy.

Billy clapped her on the back. "Have you seen her yet?"

She owed the rest of her sanity to this man. He'd been a trouper while Sellars brooded. Invited her to family dinners. Didn't kick her out after a meal when she'd surely worn out her welcome. She couldn't help it. She didn't want to leave. They were her link to Lacy. The eyes and ears. The information portal.

"No sign of her." Sellars let her gaze trickle over the faces nearby, her heart skipping.

Darlene stepped around Sellars and gave her a hug. "Hey, sweetheart. You ready to see her?"

God, how she was ready. So ready to see her. To hug her. To kiss her. To thank her. To ask if she thought about Sellars the way she thought of her. If she'd wanted Sellars the way Sellars wanted her.

She no longer wanted to throat punch the world. Thanks to Lacy.

All she wanted was a second chance at a first chance.

To walk barefoot through the grass at the Point.

To kiss Lacy under that tunnel.

And suddenly, before Sellars could answer, Lacy was in her eyesight. Across the room, standing with a guy, a bright smile on her face.

My God, could she get any more beautiful?

Sellars took a deep breath and attempted to shake the nervous tension. "There. She's right there." She nodded in Lacy's direction.

Billy squeezed her shoulder. "Why don't you let us go by and say hello while you get yourself together."

Gabby tugged the sleeve of her blazer.

Sellars bent down.

"She will bite your head off first. Ignore her until she gets it all out. All of it. You'll know because she'll take a really deep breath. Then say you're sorry. Quickly. Fast. Super fast. Got it?"

Sellars could only smile down over this sweet child. "Thanks, kiddo. Thanks!"

Gabby gave a firm nod, then grabbed Darlene's hand and pulled them across the room.

Lacy watched as Patrick dumped the donation bin for the fourth time since Shelley had unlocked those doors and invited the first person inside.

She didn't even know the denomination of those donations, only that it was huge. That it was still growing by the minute.

He turned back to look at her, his cheeks puffed out with his amazed smile. "This is beyond my expectations, Lacy. I don't know what to say."

Tears stung her eyes. She was in awe of the turnout. In awe of the future those donations held.

They'd done it. And the night had barely begun.

An accumulation of cards sat on the table beside the donation bin from local businesses who were ready and willing to help her expand this project. To push it into other states. Hopefully even farther.

"Pinch me. You need to pinch me," Lacy said.

"No pinching tonight, chick. It's real. I swear." Patrick replaced the bucket just as a man in a business suit approached. He dropped an envelope into the slot.

"Thank you so much." Lacy extended her hand to the man.

"This project was genius." He took her hand and gave a squeeze. "Absolute genius."

"I appreciate your kind words." Lacy nodded to Patrick. "This is Patrick. My partner."

Patrick extended his hand as well, and the man gave a swift shake.

"What you both have done is remarkable, and I'd love to set up a meeting with both of you. I think, no, I know, I could help you lift this off the ground."

"That would be amazing. Thank you so much!" Lacy resisted the urge to squeal her words.

She was dreaming. She had to be dreaming.

This was beyond her imagination for how this night would have turned out.

The man walked away, and Lacy scanned the walls.

Black-and-white photos dominated every inch of the room. Frames were suspended from the ceiling. Some photos were out of frames and simply clipped by clothespins on a rope that stretched from one pole to another. Antique lamps and different style lighting also created the illumination around the room, making the snapshots stand out even more.

Beautiful. The whole place was beautiful. Shelley had done an amazing job organizing these photos for display.

A woman in a tight red dress with her hair pinned in a tight bun on the crown of her head approached Lacy.

"Lacy McGowan?" the woman asked.

"Yes."

The woman pushed a folded check into her hand. "It's not much, but there is so much more waiting." She handed Patrick her business card. "And I hear you are her handy sidekick? Patrick?"

"Yes, ma'am," Patrick nearly cooed.

"I can't express enough how important it would be for us to set up a meeting with both of you." She turned back to Lacy. "I have names, big names, ready and willing to donate to your cause. Not to mention the grants. Endless grants can be at your disposal for such a worthy cause."

Lacy tried to keep her composure while she mentally screamed inside her own head.

"Make that call. Soon!" the woman said and walked away.

"I'm going to fucking faint." Lacy leaned against Patrick.

"You'll do no such thing!" Patrick playfully pushed her away. "You'll not leave me to bustle around this room all alone like the prized queen I am." He lifted his arm out, stiffened his hand, and gave a parade wave.

"Goober head."

"Aunt Lacy!"

Lacy turned to find Gabby racing toward her. She sank to her knees as Gabby dove against her.

She squeezed and squeezed, feeling her heart ache. Yes. It was an ache. She missed that child so much. Just as much as— no, more than—Billy. She was connected to this little fireball the same way she was connected to Billy. If only she could describe it.

"I have missed the hell out of you!" Lacy couldn't let her go. "So, so, so bad."

Gabby finally loosened her grip, and Lacy stood to hug Billy and Darlene.

"Everything looks amazing, Lacy." Darlene admired the photos over Lacy's head. "I had no idea there would be so many. All of them are simply incredible." She hugged Lacy again. "I'm so proud of you."

Lacy bit back her tears. Not today, dammit. "Thank you. That means a lot."

Movement caught her attention, and she turned to find Sellars standing beside her.

She could feel the smile melt from her face. Not in anger. But in complete awe. Complete lust.

Sellars looked far sexier than she had months ago. Fuck. Fuck. Fuck!

She'd rehearsed this moment. She was going to act like a mature adult. She was going to say hello. She was going to be nice and behave.

Oh, but hell no. Her body had a mind of its own, obviously, because right now, she wasn't even fucking breathing.

"Uh-oh," Gabby muttered. "She didn't bite."

"Come on, sweetheart. Let's go find something to drink." Darlene ushered Gabby and Billy away.

"Hi." Sellars held out a single rose. "Congratulations."

Lacy could only stare, feeling awkward and hot. Yes. Hot. Heat was crawling across her crotch like a phantom fog.

She couldn't tear her gaze away from Sellars's eyes. Those damn eyes.

The pressure of Patrick's body moved against her.

"I have the indescribable urge to drop to my knees and kiss your Converse tennis shoes right now," Patrick said. "You've rendered her speechless. It's a miracle!"

"Shut the fuck up, Patrick," Lacy said, her sights still locked on Sellars.

"That's okay. I don't need an introduction." Patrick pushed his hand out to Sellars. "You would have to be the one and only Kip Sellars."

Sellars finally dragged her sights from Lacy's face to Patrick's outstretched hand. She gave it a firm shake and moved her attention right back on Lacy.

She didn't have a choice. Right now, she had a one-track mind. The same as it was yesterday. Days before. Last week. Last month. One track. One Lacy. And now that Lacy was in the flesh only feet away from her, she didn't want to look at anything but her. Not at the remarkable photos all around the room. Not at the food lined against the back wall. Not at the wine fountain.

Just Lacy. Only Lacy.

Her insides ached. Her stomach knotted. Her heart sputtered.

God. She was beautiful in her bright white business suit with the arms cut out. The matching pants that were loose around her legs but pressed against the curve of those hips like a lover's hold. Not to mention those black pumps. The very ones she'd love to have dangling over her shoulders. They were spiked and sexy and gave Lacy an extra few inches. Just enough inches so that Sellars wouldn't have to bend so far to reach those lips.

Oh, but she'd love to hover over her while her fingers spread and filled her.

The urge to kiss her was strong. Unbearable, actually.

It was all she could do to contain her impulse. And getting harder as Lacy stared at her.

"Okay, well, I'm feeling like I'm about to watch porn in the middle of a movie theater," Patrick said. "I think I'll go, um, check for dust in a corner or something."

As soon as Patrick turned his back, Sellars took another step toward Lacy. She'd never met a woman who could make her insides melt with simple eye contact.

She was so in love with this woman. So fearful she'd screwed it all up.

All she could do was pray something she had tonight would win Lacy over. She wasn't sure how to live the rest of her life knowing she'd lost something so special. Someone so perfect for her.

"You look amazing."

Lacy struggled to find her voice. To find her tongue. To find anything besides the wet heat stirring between her thighs. What the hell was wrong with her? Where had her composure vanished to?

Fucking say something!

"Thank you." Lacy finally forced out the words.

"The place looks incredible. I had no idea your project was so...intense."

Lacy nodded, her gaze dropping to Sellars's lips.

She wanted to throw herself against Sellars. Wanted to wrap her legs around that tight body and grind. Yes. Grind. She wanted to grind until an orgasm brought her voice back. Or took it away for a damn better reason than simply staring at someone she hadn't been able to rip out of her head for months now.

Sellars pushed the rose farther out, and Lacy remembered that she was supposed to take it.

Lacy reached out and took the stem.

Sellars held on to it and bent down farther. "I left my demon at the finish line."

Lacy tried to smile, to show her she could hear her, that she was aware of her presence, but she didn't trust herself to say anything. Anything that wasn't sarcastic, that was. Or begging. Right now, she could beg.

She opened her mouth to force out a response, praying it would be polite. That she didn't let her dirty thoughts roll out with her words. To simply say she was sorry, although she wasn't, but for some reason, she wanted to say those words. Had to say them.

"I'm sorry to interrupt this…very heated moment," Patrick said, ripping the apology from her mouth. "But he was looking for you."

Lacy finally looked away from Sellars to find Ralph smiling at her.

"Ralph!" Lacy looked him up and down, taking in his new clothing, jeans, T-shirt, and blazer, as well as his styled new haircut. "You look absolutely handsome!"

Sellars smiled. "He looks sharp, right?"

Lacy glanced from Sellars, then back to Ralph. "You look…you look like Sellars."

"That's what happens when you have a roommate." Sellars winked at Ralph. "Well, ex roomie now."

"He's what?" Lacy looked between them, trying to absorb what she'd heard.

"Ralph's been living with me until a few weeks ago. He's living at the hotel now."

Lacy swung her gaze back to Ralph for confirmation.

He nodded and gave a timid shrug. "Sellars got me a job at the cemetery."

"A cemetery?" Lacy looked to Sellars, not trusting herself not to break down in tears right now.

Ralph was the best guy ever. Meeting him at the soup kitchen, hearing his story, was what had prompted her entire project. She'd wanted to know more. Wanted to see inside their world. His world.

Our World Through Their Eyes was alive because of Ralph.

"Yes. Not just him. Several others so far. More cemeteries and mortuaries, other places that I've reached out to in the past month, have already agreed to open spots for people like Ralph."

"People like Ralph?" Lacy arched a brow. She felt the defensive bite in her words.

"Yes. People *just* like Ralph," Sellars said. "People like you, like me, who just need someone to help them see the light. To shake the demon."

Lacy considered her words, decided there was no malice intended in them, besides the fact that she was daring Lacy to argue with her, and turned back to Ralph. "You live at the hotel?"

"Yes, ma'am. Mr. Reynolds booked the entire top floor for each of us who are working."

Lacy wanted to cry. She wanted to hug him.

Hell, she wanted to hug Sellars.

"Actually, you paid for it," Sellars said. "With the money you wouldn't take from my grandfather. He told me about your deal, by the way. That the money was never going to you, that you requested him to pay for an art show. Like this one. For them."

Tears stung her eyes. To know that Ralph was now off the streets. That some of his friends were as well. That more could be following. Her heart swelled, and a lump rose in her throat. She looked down and pep-talked herself out of crying.

Not tonight, dammit!

"Okay, well, Ralph, want to see your section?" Patrick blurted when silence fell around them.

Ralph stepped toward Lacy, and she looked up through blurry eyes. "There's no one like you on earth. You're special, Miss Lacy."

Lacy hugged him tight then watched him walk toward the side of the room.

When she turned back to Sellars, she was closer, staring down over Lacy like a prized possession.

"Did you tell my grandfather to hug me?" Sellars cocked an eyebrow up. "It was kind of creepy."

Lacy could only stare at her, too many things to say locked in her mind, so many things she knew she shouldn't say right now. Right now wasn't the time.

Right now she wanted to crawl into Sellers's arms. Just one more time, she wanted to feel Sellars's weight pinning her down. Just one more fucking time.

"You did that for them?"

"Of course," Sellars said. "Everyone has their own demon. Some just need a little extra help fighting them."

Lacy nodded, the need to kiss Sellars overwhelming. She looked away to help control the urge.

Sellars stepped even closer. She cupped Lacy's chin with her index finger and tipped her head back, forcing Lacy to make eye contact.

"Will you kiss me now? Please? I've been working very hard to deserve it."

Lacy stared into those tranquil eyes and saw a future waiting for her on the other side. A future she never wanted. A future she never thought she could ever want. But there it was. In all its glorious form, from the bad to the worse, from the good to the better, it was within her reach.

There wasn't a fucking thing on earth she wanted more than to kiss this woman right now.

She flung her arms around Sellars's neck and crushed their lips together.

From somewhere in the back of the room, she heard Gabby squeal with delight.

Her heart swelled as Sellars wrapped her arms around Lacy's waist and pulled her closer.

For everything that had ever felt so wrong in her life, this minute evaporated all of them.

Demons. Gone. Fear. Vanished.

Love. Landed.

Lacy possessively tightened her grip around Sellars's neck.

Forever, she wanted to hug and kiss her. Forever, she wanted to give her a hard time, on purpose, so Sellars would be forced to put her in her place. Sexually. Every day.

And the way Sellars was holding on to her, kissing her, she wanted the same thing. Her actions with Ralph, out of the kindness of her heart, out of love, proved she wanted the same things.

Sellars kissed her harder as the claps sounded around them.

Later, when they were naked, on a mattress, depleted of oxygen, she'd let Sellars know that swear jars would be banned from their home.

And that forever and ever, she would be at that finish line waiting for her.

The End

About the Author

Larkin Rose lives in a "blink and you've missed it" town with Rose, her wife of twenty-two years, in the beautiful state of South Carolina. Together, they shared seven very active kids who weren't allowed to read her books until they were married. They are now all grown up, married, and multiplied, making her a super Nana to eleven grandkids, too. They are still not allowed to read her books (or rather, admit it). After a four-year hiatus, she's now back writing full time.

The fantasies continue. The clatter of keys continues. And the birth of erotic creations shall carry on.

To know more, visit Larinrose.com.

Books Available from Bold Strokes Books

Dangerous Curves by Larkin Rose. When love waits at the finish line, dangerous curves are a risk worth taking. (978-1-63555-353-6)

Love to the Rescue by Radclyffe. Can two people who share a past really be strangers? (978-1-62639-973-0)

Love's Portrait by Anna Larner. When museum curator Molly Goode and benefactor Georgina Wright uncover a portrait's secret, public and private truths are exposed, and their deepening love hangs in the balance. (978-1-63555-057-3)

Model Behavior by MJ Williamz. Can one woman's instability shatter a new couple's dreams of happiness? (978-1-63555-379-6)

Pretending in Paradise by M. Ullrich. When travelwisdom. com assigns PR specialist Caroline Beckett and travel blogger Emma Morgan to cover a hot new couples retreat, they're forced to fake a relationship to secure a reservation. (978-1-63555-399-4)

Recipe for Love by Aurora Rey. Hannah Little doesn't have much use for fancy chefs or fancy restaurants, but when New York City chef Drew Davis comes to town, their attraction just might be a recipe for love. (978-1-63555-367-3)

Survivor's Guilt and Other Stories by Greg Herren. Award-winning author Greg Herren's short stories are finally pulled together into a single collection, including the Macavity Award nominated title story and the first-ever Chanse MacLeod short story. (978-1-63555-413-7)

The House by Eden Darry. After a vicious assault, Sadie, Fin, and their family retreat to a house they think is the perfect place to start over, until they realize not all is as it seems. (978-1-63555-395-6)

Uninvited by Jane C. Esther. When Aerin McLeary's body becomes host for an alien intent on invading Earth, she must work with researcher Olivia Ando to uncover the truth and save humankind. (978-1-63555-282-9)

Comrade Cowgirl by Yolanda Wallace. When cattle rancher Laramie Bowman accepts a lucrative job offer far from home, will her heart end up getting lost in translation? (978-1-63555-375-8)

Double Vision by Ellie Hart. When her cell phone rings, Giselle Cutler answers it—and finds herself speaking to a dead woman. (978-1-63555-385-7)

Inheritors of Chaos by Barbara Ann Wright. As factions splinter and reunite, will anyone survive the final showdown between gods and mortals on an alien world? (978-1-63555-294-2)

Love on Lavender Lane by Karis Walsh. Accompanied by the buzz of honeybees and the scent of lavender, Paige and Kassidy must find a way to compromise on their approach to business if they want to save Lavender Lane Farm—and find a way to make room for love along the way. (978-1-63555-286-7)

Spinning Tales by Brey Willows. When the fairy tale begins to unravel and villains are on the loose, will Maggie and Kody be able to spin a new tale? (978-1-63555-314-7)

The Do-Over by Georgia Beers. Bella Hunt has made a good life for herself and put the past behind her. But when the bane of her high school existence shows up for Bella's class on conflict resolution, the last thing they expect is to fall in love. (978-1-63555-393-2)

What Happens When by Samantha Boyette. For Molly Kennan, senior year is already an epic disaster, and falling for mysterious waitress Zia is about to make life a whole lot worse. (978-1-63555-408-3)

Wooing the Farmer by Jenny Frame. When fiercely independent modern socialite Penelope Huntingdon-Stewart and traditional country farmer Sam McQuade meet, trusting their hearts is harder than it looks. (978-1-63555-381-9)

A Chapter on Love by Laney Webber. When Jannika and Lee reunite, their instant connection feels like a gift, but neither is ready for a second chance at love. Will they finally get on the same page when it comes to love? (978-1-63555-366-6)

Drawing Down the Mist by Sheri Lewis Wohl. Everyone thinks Grand Duchess Maria Romanova died in 1918. They were almost right. (978-1-63555-341-3)

Listen by Kris Bryant. Lily Croft is inexplicably drawn to Hope D'Marco but will she have the courage to confront the consequences of her past and present colliding? (978-1-63555-318-5)

Perfect Partners by Maggie Cummings. Elite police dog trainer Sara Wright has no intention of falling in love with a coworker, until Isabel Marquez arrives at Homeland Security's Northeast Regional Training facility and Sara's good intentions start to falter. (978-1-63555-363-5)

Shut Up and Kiss Me by Julie Cannon. What better way to spend two weeks of hell in paradise than in the company of a hot, sexy woman? (978-1-63555-343-7)

Spencer's Cove by Missouri Vaun. When Foster Owen and Abigail Spencer meet they uncover a story of lives adrift, loves lost, and true love found. (978-1-63555-171-6)

Without Pretense by TJ Thomas. After living for decades hiding from the truth, can Ava learn to trust Bianca with her secrets and her heart? (978-1-63555-173-0)

Unexpected Lightning by Cass Sellars. Lightning strikes once more when Sydney and Parker fight a dangerous stranger who threatens the peace they both desperately want. (978-1-163555-276-8)

Emily's Art and Soul by Joy Argento. When Emily meets Andi Marino she thinks she's found a new best friend but Emily doesn't know that Andi is fast falling in love with her.

Caught up in exploring her sexuality, will Emily see the only woman she needs is right in front of her? (978-1-63555-355-0)

Escape to Pleasure: Lesbian Travel Erotica edited by Sandy Lowe and Victoria Villasenor. Join these award-winning authors as they explore the sensual side of erotic lesbian travel. (978-1-63555-339-0)

Music City Dreamers by Robyn Nyx. Music can bring lovers together. In Music City, it can tear them apart. (978-1-63555-207-2)

Ordinary is Perfect by D. Jackson Leigh. Atlanta marketing superstar Autumn Swan's life derails when she inherits a country home, a child, and a very interesting neighbor. (978-1-63555-280-5)

Royal Court by Jenny Frame. When royal dresser Holly Weaver's passionate personality begins to melt Royal Marine Captain Quincy's icy heart, will Holly be ready for what she exposes beneath? (978-1-63555-290-4)

Strings Attached by Holly Stratimore. Success. Riches. Music. Passion. It's a life most can only dream of, but stardom comes at a cost. (978-1-63555-347-5)

The Ashford Place by Jean Copeland. When Isabelle Ashford inherits an old house in small-town Connecticut, family secrets, a shocking discovery, and an unexpected romance complicate her plan for a fast profit and a temporary stay. (978-1-63555-316-1)

Treason by Gun Brooke. Zoem Malderyn's existence is a deadly threat to everyone on Gemocon and Commander Neenja KahSandra must find a way to save the woman she loves from having to commit the ultimate sacrifice. (978-1-63555-244-7)

A Wish Upon a Star by Jeannie Levig. Erica Cooper has learned to depend on only herself, but when her new neighbor, Leslie Raymond, befriends Erica's special needs daughter, the walls protecting her heart threaten to crumble. (978-1-63555-274-4)

Answering the Call by Ali Vali. Detective Sept Savoie returns to the streets of New Orleans, as do the dead bodies from ritualistic killings, and she does everything in her power to bring them to justice while trying to keep her partner, Keegan Blanchard, safe. (978-1-63555-050-4)

Breaking Down Her Walls by Erin Zak. Could a love worth staying for be the key to breaking down Julia Finch's walls? (978-1-63555-369-7)

Exit Plans for Teenage Freaks by 'Nathan Burgoine. Cole always has a plan—especially for escaping his small-town reputation as "that kid who was kidnapped when he was four"— but when he teleports to a museum, it's time to face facts: it's possible he's a total freak after all. (978-1-63555-098-6)

Friends Without Benefits by Dena Blake. When Dex Putman gets the woman she thought she always wanted, she soon wonders if it's really love after all. (978-1-63555-349-9)

Invalid Evidence by Stevie Mikayne. Private Investigator Jil Kidd is called away to investigate a possible killer whale, just when her partner Jess needs her most. (978-1-63555-307-9)

Pursuit of Happiness by Carsen Taite. When attorney Stevie Palmer's client reveals a scandal that could derail Senator Meredith Mitchell's presidential bid, their chance at love may be collateral damage. (978-1-63555-044-3)

Seascape by Karis Walsh. Marine biologist Tess Hansen returns to Washington's isolated northern coast where she struggles to adjust to small-town living while courting an endowment for her orca research center from Brittany James. (978-1-63555-079-5)

Second in Command by VK Powell. Jazz Perry's life is disrupted and her career jeopardized when she becomes personally involved with the case of an abandoned child and the child's competent but strict social worker, Emory Blake. (978-1-63555-185-3)

Taking Chances by Erin McKenzie. When Valerie Cruz and Paige Wellington clash over what's in the best interest of the children in Valerie's care, the children may be the ones who teach them it's worth taking chances for love. (978-1-63555-209-6)